& Resolutions

...Plus!

CAN YOU HANDLE SCANDAL?
TRY OUR FAB QUIZ AT
THE BACK OF THE BOOK

SOME SECRETS ARE JUST TOO GOOD TO KEEP
TO YOURSELF!

Sugar Secrets...

Sugar
SECRETS...

...& Resolutions

Mel Sparke

Collins

An Imprint of HarperCollinsPublishers

Published in Great Britain by Collins in 2000
Collins is an imprint of HarperCollins*Publishers* Ltd
77–85 Fulham Palace Road, Hammersmith, London W6 8JB

The HarperCollins website address is
www.**fire**and**water**.com

9 8 7 6 5 4 3 2 1

Creative consultant: Karen McCombie
Copyright © Sugar 2000. Licensed with TLC

ISBN 0 00 675430 9

Printed and bound in Great Britain by
Caledonian International Book Manufacturing Ltd, Glasgow

Conditions of Sale

CHAPTER 1

● ●

HAPPY NEW YEAR!

He was so lost in her smile that it took a moment to realise she was moving towards him. Stunned, he found himself automatically tilting his head in readiness for what was about to happen. He could hardly believe that it *was* going to happen – after all this time. But the way her eyes were softly closing, the way her mouth was forming into a perfect, tender pout... there was no doubting what was she was about to do.

And when the kiss finally came – her lips gently touching, pressing against his – it was as if his whole body had dissolved in happiness. Instead of muscle, there was rubber. Instead of bone, there was warm candle wax. He felt as light and buoyant and weightless as if he were floating star-shaped on his back in a tropical lagoon.

With no bidding from him, his arms were just about to wrap themselves around her and draw her closer, closer to him. His lips were just about to part, letting him sink further into her kiss...

And then she broke away.

"Happy New Year!" she beamed at him.

"Happy New Y—" he tried to respond, but he'd already lost Kerry's attention to Sonja Harvey, who was whooping and jumping about in excitement.

All around Joe Gladwin, hundreds of other revellers were just as caught up in the joyful madness that had erupted after the midnight chimes. But for Joe, the mayhem and the music of the party might as well have been something that was happening on the telly, he felt so distanced from it. Standing still and inwardly silent, he let the memory of his first real kiss with Kerry Bellamy linger on.

All half a second of it.

"C'mere, gorgeous!" said a voice in his ear and his head was caught in a vice-like armlock. "Mmmmmmm-*wah*!"

Joe's second New Year kiss wasn't quite as delicate as the first, but was nearly as memorable because of its sheer force.

Releasing her grip on Joe, Catrina Osgood ruffled his hair carelessly and disappeared into the crowds of party-goers in search of another face to suction.

Joe blushed furiously, glad of the muted lighting in the cavernous town hall. Cat might not have thought anything of her overenthusiastic slobber (just one of many she'd be dishing out), but it had suddenly reminded Joe of his recent bout of madness – when he'd thought for all of five minutes that he actually fancied Catrina.

To be fair, shy boy Joe hadn't *totally* acted out of character when he felt a faint stirring of attraction towards his louder-than-loud mate; she'd apparently gone through a personality transplant, turning from the Wicked Witch of Winstead into something altogether more sweet and gentle.

Of course, it wasn't what it had seemed. By sheer fluke, Cat had landed the part of Cinderella in her college Christmas pantomime. It had taken a while for Joe to twig that the sweetness 'n' light change in Cat's personality was simply her getting into character for her starring role.

But this New Year's Eve, it seemed that it wasn't only Joe who was feeling awkward as the party poppers erupted all around him, sending streamers flying into the air.

Wonder what's going on there? he asked himself, his eyes settling on a strange encounter between Matt and Anna.

Matt Ryan, with one arm still circled round his girlfriend Gabrielle Adjani's waist, had turned around with a grin on his face, obviously ready to bellow a Happy New Year at whoever was close by. At that same second, Anna Michaels – fresh from giving her brother Owen a hug – turned to do the same.

They were so close to each other, they could have kissed without taking a step nearer, but instead of reaching out instinctively and doing just that, Joe noticed that they both faltered, smiles slipping, before Anna moved forward stiffly and gave Matt a brief, self-conscious peck on the cheek.

Almost immediately, they swung their attention away from one another, casting desperate glances around for someone else to fix on. Or so it appeared to Joe, locked in his own little world of self-consciousness just a few feet away.

"Joe!" smiled Maya Joshi, bringing him back to earth. "I was just saying to the others that we should dip out and get some fresh air – it's too hot and mad in here!"

"Uh, OK," agreed Joe dubiously.

He certainly wasn't feeling at his most relaxed; his two kisses had left him pretty disconcerted (for different reasons) but he hadn't expected to be leaving the party quite so soon.

Maya spotted the confusion in his face and tried to spell things out a little more clearly.

"I don't mean we should go home, Joe. It's just that Matt says the door to the fire escape behind the DJ booth is open," she explained, motioning towards the black curtain behind the speakers and console where the music was blasting out. "We can sneak away for a bit – sit on the fire escape and, y'know, just hang out, all of us."

Maya hid her sentimental side pretty well most of the time, but it was most definitely there, Joe knew, lurking not too far under the surface. And gathering all her friends together at such an auspicious moment – the very start of a whole new year – was a typical Maya gesture. No dramatic pronouncements of affection or over-the-top clinginess, just enjoying the sense of belonging.

"Great idea," he grinned at her.

"Well, come on – help me round up the troops..." she grinned back, linking her arm into his.

• • •

"Anna says that if you look up at the sky just after midnight at New Year, it'll tell you what kind of year you're going to have," said Maya, tossing her shiny dark hair back and staring up into the deep, star-spangled indigo night above them.

"Pity she's not here to interpret it then, isn't it?" murmured Joe, squinting upwards.

"She'll be here – she was trying to track down Owen and Sonja, remember?"

Joe nodded wordlessly. The others had all promised faithfully that they'd follow Maya and Joe out on to the fire escape – as soon as they'd finished talking to people/gone to the loo/got another round of drinks in or (in Cat's case) had snogged any male between the ages of sixteen and twenty-three. (And there were a few hundred of those in the building for her to work her way around.)

"So what do *you* think the sky's trying to tell us?" Joe asked his friend, aware of her shivering slightly as she sat next to him on the open metal staircase.

"Well," answered Maya slowly, "I guess that with so many stars out, it means it's going to be a bright, exciting year. There are a couple of clouds over there though, see?"

"Uh-huh," Joe responded, following her finger.

"So I think that means there are a few hassles on the horizon, but since the wind's blowing them quickly across the sky, those troubles won't stick around for long."

"So clouds are bad, are they?"

"Not necessarily."

"What if we'd come out here and the whole sky was just a mass of clouds?"

"I'd say that it was going to be an interesting year, with lots of unexpected surprises hidden away."

"Maya, you're just making this up, aren't you?" Joe laughed.

"Totally," agreed Maya. "I haven't got a clue, really. Where *is* Anna when you need her?"

"Probably waiting for Owen and Sonja to come up for air long enough for her to drag them out here."

Sonja hadn't expected to see her long-distance love for another few weeks, but Owen had sprung a surprise, lightning visit on her earlier that evening, landing up on her doorstep as she and the other girls were getting ready for the party. In between bouncing off the walls with excitement for the night and the boy, she'd been practically smothering Owen with kisses.

Not that he seemed to be complaining.

"Well, Joe, I guess we'd better start without the others..." said Maya, changing the subject. Though what to, Joe wasn't sure.

"Start?" he asked warily.

"Resolutions. That's the typical question to

ask, isn't it? " said Maya, looking at her friend with her dark brown almond eyes. "So what's yours?"

"Mine? I, uh..." Joe waffled, not sure what to say.

"OK, I'll go first. I would love for something amazing to happen with my photography this year."

"You did pretty well with it last year," said Joe of the year that was all of fifteen minutes in the past already. "You came second in that big competition, didn't you?"

Maya nodded, remembering with pride the shocking moment when she was called on to the podium to collect second prize at the art centre the previous summer.

"I know, but I'm not going to give up there!" she smiled. "Joining the photography club was one of the best things I've ever done – I just feel so positive about it. I know something really good's going to come out of it."

Joe was suddenly struck with inspiration.

"Driving!" he blurted out. "I want to learn to drive this year."

"That would be cool," said Maya encouragingly. "Then we wouldn't have to rely on Matt for lifts everywhere!"

"Only one problem, of course," grinned Joe wryly.

"What?"

"I can't afford lessons and if I could, I wouldn't be able to afford even an old banger at the end of it."

Maya understood the situation. Money was fairly tight at home for Joe, since his parents had split up several years before. And filling in on the odd shift at the End-of-the-Line café didn't exactly bring in a whole lot of cash for him either.

"Another thing..." he continued.

Maya gazed at her friend, patiently waiting to hear what he had to say.

"...that's not even my real resolution."

"What is it then?" asked Maya, noting the nervous grin twitching at Joe's mouth.

"I, uh..." Joe turned to make sure they were still alone, before continuing quietly. "I kind of made this vow that I was going to give up holding out for Kerry..."

Maya reached over for his hand and gave it a squeeze. She was the only one of the crowd who knew that Joe had been lost in love for his friend. And Maya also knew as well as Joe did how pointless that love was, since Kerry and Ollie were such a solid, happy item.

"I'm pleased, Joe," she reassured him. "It won't be easy, but I think it's probably better if you did move on and find someone else."

"That's the trouble," he shrugged. "I've been trying to think like this for quite a while now – New Year was just a good way of finally putting a lid on it. And then..."

"What?"

"And then she kissed me tonight..." he sighed heavily, every scrap of breath wistfully pouring from his soul.

"Oh, Joe," smiled Maya sadly, cuddling her friend in her arms.

Getting over Kerry is going to be harder than I thought, Joe realised, glancing up at the rogue clouds in the sky.

CHAPTER 2

●●●●●●●●●●●●●●●●●●●●●●●●●●

JUST DON'T ASK...

Please don't ask me, please don't ask me!
Kerry chanted a silent mantra to herself,
frantically twirling the tiny stones on her chakra
necklace.

"Anna's next!" chirped Sonja, extricating one
arm from around Owen for long enough to point
at his sister.

All the friends (with the exception of Cat, last
seen with her arms draped around the two Dutch
boys who had been hanging around the café and
the band for the last few weeks) had joined Maya
and Joe out on the fire escape. The three couples
– Ollie and Kerry, Sonja and Owen, Matt and
Gabrielle – were using the chill night air as an
excuse to cuddle closer as they perched on
the fire escape.

Anna, who'd walked up a few of the iron steps and settled herself behind Maya and Joe, thought for a moment before speaking.

"OK, I guess my resolution would be to have a peaceful year," she smiled.

"You old hippy!" Ollie laughed, unaware of the traumas in Anna's past that made her resolution so meaningful.

"And what's yours, Mr Sarkypants?" Sonja quizzed him. "To finally give up on that glorified rusty hairdryer of yours and sell it for scrap?"

"Oi!" protested Ollie Stanton. "That Vespa is worth a lot of money – or at least it will be if I ever manage to get it running for more than five minutes at a time..."

Without turning to look at him as he stood behind her, Kerry could sense Ollie's genuine hurt, despite his joking. Restoring the old (or 'vintage', as Ollie preferred) moped was a bit of a pet project of his, although it seemed to spend more time broken down in the shed behind his parents' pub, waiting for yet another expensive spare part, than actually out on the road.

"Tell us, then – what *is* your resolution, Ol?" Kerry prompted him quickly, to put a stop to Sonja's misjudged teasing.

"Isn't it obvious?" he asked, giving her a squeeze around the waist.

What does he mean? Kerry's mind raced. *That me and him should stay together this year?*

"The band!" Ollie blurted out. "I just want The Loud to go from strength to strength!"

"What — like get a *proper* manager, you mean?" joked Joe.

Ollie's Uncle Nick, owner of the End-of-the-Line café, had volunteered himself as manager of his nephew's band. And though he'd done really well for them so far, including getting them a regular weekly spot at the Railway Tavern, there was still something about him that the lads couldn't take seriously.

Maybe it was the fact that he wore his hair in a ponytail, despite a rapidly growing bald spot on top. Or maybe it was his tendency to exaggerate just what big mates he was with rock stars — all because he'd worked as a roadie for a few groups when he was younger.

"Hey, don't knock Nick!" Maya scolded the snickering boys, then started giggling herself when she realised how stupid her words had sounded.

Kerry slipped what she hoped was a convincing smile on her face but couldn't help feeling disappointed that Ollie's resolution had nothing to do with her after all.

What would he think of mine? she wondered to herself, feeling the heat of his breath on her neck and the vibration of his chest against her back as he laughed. *Would he think I was being stupid? I know Sonja would. So would Maya. As for my parents... Oh God!*

She must have shuddered involuntarily and Ollie curled his arms even tighter around her.

"All right, Kez?" he whispered quietly, his floppy brown hair tickling the side of her face.

"Mmm," she nodded, covering his arms with her own.

But the resolution-spilling was still going on and their intimate moment was gone in a flash.

"Sonja! What's yours?" asked Maya, pulling the sleeves of her top down over her fingers to keep them warm.

"Yeah, what's yours, Son?" Ollie bellowed in Kerry's ear, obviously keen to get his revenge. "Maybe to make it in the modelling game?"

Sonja could handle herself, but Kerry felt this was a pretty low blow and stuck her elbow back into Ollie's stomach to let him know. After all, it had only been a couple of months since Sonja had made a bit of a fool of herself, boasting to the others about how easy it would be for her to get into modelling.

With her athletic figure, Scandinavian colouring and bags of confidence, Sonja might feasibly have been model material. But she'd nearly found herself signed to a local agency who kept the models on their books busy all right – with jobs advertising cut-price plumbing contractors and tyre warehouses. Sonja's glamorous expectations of modelling for some of the top names in the country had vanished at about the same time as her pride had taken a tumble.

"I'm going to ignore that remark," said Sonja with dignity. "And the answer is, my resolution would be to get into my first choice course this year."

"Ooh, very worthy," laughed Matt, who had had more than enough of education after the years he'd spent at boarding school. All the recent talk among his friends about choosing college and university places just left him cold.

He was thankful for the fact that Ollie, like him, had chosen the working route. Even if neither of them was exactly setting the career world alight...

Another thing eighteen-year-old Matt was grateful for at times like these – even though it had caused him major doubts when he first found out – was that his girlfriend Gabrielle was still only fourteen. She had vague notions of what she wanted to do, but certainly felt the decision was so far off that it wasn't uppermost in her topics of conversation. Unlike Sonja, Joe and Kerry, who'd all be leaving sixth form this summer. Although he had to admit that Kerry, bless her, hadn't said much about it and bored the pants off him like her best friend had.

"So this first choice course – where's that then?" asked Owen, looking intrigued. Only catching up with Sonja now and again and not being 'officially' girlfriend and boyfriend, he wasn't privy to *all* the day-to-day goings-on in her life.

Even though Kerry was preoccupied with counting how many of her friends were left with resolutions untold (Matt, Gabrielle, Owen and herself), she was strangely surprised at the way Sonja suddenly acted as if she hadn't heard a word Owen had said, despite being draped around him like a comfort blanket.

"Gaby? What's your resolution?" Sonja asked with overenthusiastic perkiness.

Gabrielle twirled one of her beaded plaits around between her fingers and looked up at Matt soulfully.

"I don't think I've really got one," she giggled nervously.

"Course you have – everyone has!" Sonja tried to cajole her. "Matt has, haven't you?"

"Nope," shrugged Matt.

His father had asked the same question a few hours earlier when they'd shared a rare dinner together before doing their own thing – his father hosting a New Year party in their huge house for a select band of business associates and golf club buddies, and Matt DJing at the town hall's New Year bash, supporting the semi-celebrity DJ who was headlining.

When his father had asked that question, Matt knew that the response his father was secretly hoping for was along the lines of, "Yes, Dad, I've made a resolution – and it's to give up this DJing lark and get a proper job."

But Matt was certain he'd disappointed him. His answer had been the same one he'd just given Sonja.

"Kez!" cried Sonja, as she stopped glowering at Matt for being such a spoilsport and turned, just as her best mate had dreaded, towards her. "Tell, tell, tell!"

Kerry felt a cold sweat break out on her body, while a hot flush spread across her lightly freckle-speckled face. She hadn't known it was possible for those two sensations to happen simultaneously.

"I suppose..." she began, aware that Sonja expected some half-decent response from her. "I suppose it's the same as Anna's – a peaceful year."

"Nah-*aah*!" honked Sonja, doing an impersonation of a 'wrong' buzzer on a quiz show. "Not good enough – you can't copy someone else's answer."

"Well," Kerry flustered, racking her brains for something that would pacify Sonja, "then I guess that it would be... to be happy."

"Wow, that's lame!" teased Sonja.

"I think it's lovely," Ollie contradicted, kissing Kerry on the cheek.

She hoped she wasn't as hot as she felt – Ollie's lips would be burnt if the temperature she felt inside was truly reflected on her skin.

A clatter of shoes on the metal staircase turned everyone's attention towards the fire escape door, and Kerry was relieved to see Cat – her trademark lipstick shockingly absent as a result of copious kissing – teetering towards her friends.

"I thought I'd lost you!" she said petulantly, making her way over to them, squeezing past Maya and Joe and settling herself companionably next to Anna.

"We thought you were too busy making lots of new friends to come and join your old ones," Sonja laughingly jibed her cousin.

"Me?" squeaked Cat, all innocence. "It's New Year – it's against the law not to kiss strangers, isn't it?"

"Yeah, yeah," said Ollie with a well-intentioned dollop of sarcasm. "So, Cat, now you've finally decided to hang out with us, entertain us with your New Year's resolution, why don't you?"

Even Kerry couldn't wait to hear this one. Cat's wily mind worked in strange ways and since her latest crusade was to become a TV or movie actress (the cheesier and more glamorous the better), her resolution was bound to be something along the lines of having her own Ricki Lake-style chat show before the year was out. That or selling her 'story' to *OK!*

"My resolution?" she replied, staring wistfully at the skies above her. "My resolution... my absolute dream, really..."

"Get on with it!" Sonja hurried her up, sure Catrina was just milking the drama of the moment for as much as she could.

Cat shot Sonja a dirty look before raising her eyes to the stars once again.

"If I could wish for anything this year..." she began, a slight tremor in her voice.

Kerry strained to see her more clearly in the darkness – she was sure she could see a glint of tears in Cat's eyes, illuminated by a shaft of light leaking through the fire escape door.

"...more than anything..."

Sonja yawned loudly.

"...I'd like someone to ask me to marry them."

It was such a great performance that the others weren't sure whether to laugh – or give a round of applause.

CHAPTER 3

• •

RING, RING

The cold had finally driven them all shivering back into the cavernous town hall, which had been transformed from a staid civic function area into a balloon-filled, strobe-lit venue for the night.

"I've got to say, I don't think much of your resolution, Cat," said Maya as the two girls followed their crowd to the edge of the dance floor.

"Oh? Why?" asked Cat. Her arms were crossed defensively over her chest and her eyes were racing around the faces in the hall in irritation – doing her best to look anywhere but at Maya, especially if she was about to deliver a lecture.

"Well, it's not very girl power, is it?" Maya continued, twisting and turning her way through the crowds. "You're only just seventeen! You've got all these plans and schemes and ambitions in your head and you come out with this ridiculous statement about wanting to get *married*?"

"Maya, get off my case," Cat muttered, her face still turned away from her friend.

"And another thing," Maya went on, "what are you playing at with Marc and Rudi? How can you say you'd love to do something serious like get married, when you act the complete opposite, flirting outrageously with both those lads, when you couldn't care less about either of them?"

"What are you saying, Maya?" sighed Cat, desperate to get back to the party.

Maya knew she was annoying her friend, but *someone* had to tell Cat when she was in danger of going too far – and the only one who dared to do it without her going into meltdown was Maya.

"Cat, all I'm saying is have a bit more respect for yourself. Don't hold on to this romantic notion that a man will sort your life out. And don't try and find him by snogging the entire male population of Winstead – plus passing Dutch visitors – when you couldn't give a damn about any of them."

"Oh, yeah?" said Cat, narrowing her eyes and finally focusing a gimlet stare on Maya. "Well, you know what I think? I think you've contradicted yourself, Miss Know-all Joshi. '*Don't* get too serious!' 'Don't flirt!' Aren't they the exact opposite pieces of advice? Anyway, I think your trouble is you're jealous!"

"Jealous?" Maya laughed. "How come?"

"You fancy Rudi yourself. Didn't you snog him at Enigma on Christmas Eve?"

"Cat, *he* kissed *me*. And you know that the only reason he did it was because *you* told him I fancied him!"

"Well, that's very convenient to say, isn't it?"

"Cat," said Maya flatly, not rising to the bait, "did it ever occur to you to write a book instead of being an actress?"

Cat looked at her friend blankly.

"You're just wasting that imagination of yours," Maya shrugged. "You should write all your wild ideas on paper. You'd make a million..."

• • •

Matt watched Gabrielle with obvious pride as she talked excitedly with a passing friend.

"Isn't she beautiful?" he said to Ollie beside him, without taking his eyes off his girlfriend.

Ollie looked over at Gabrielle and nodded. "Yeah, she's really pretty, Matt. But so's Kerry. Do you want to get into a game of My Girlfriend's Better Than Your Girlfriend or something?"

"Nope," Matt grinned, staring at Gabrielle's dark-skinned profile. "I know I'd win."

"Oi!" Ollie protested, landing a mock punch in Matt's stomach. In a perfectly choreographed matey response, Matt pretended to double up.

"You know something though?" he said, straightening up and looking serious.

"What's that?" asked Ollie, pushing his hair from his eyes, which was pretty pointless since it always landed right back in the same floppy style.

"Something Cat said got me thinking tonight." Matt leaned closer, as if what he was saying was top-secret, classified, for-Ollie's-ears-only information.

"Oooh, I don't like the sound of that," Ollie replied, scrunching up his nose.

"Nah, wait," Matt tried to explain himself. "It was when she said she wanted someone to ask her to marry him..."

"Don't do it!" Ollie joked. "I won't let you make such a sacrifice as marrying Cat!"

"Not Cat! *Gaby*, you idiot!"

Ollie looked as if he'd just watched his Vespa go through a crusher.

"You want to ask Gaby to *marry* you? But you're only eighteen, Matt. And she's not legally allowed to buy herself a pint for another four years, apart from anything else—"

"Hold up!" interrupted Matt, suddenly

realising what Ollie thought he meant. "I'm not talking about actually getting *married* or anything, you nutter. Just a commitment thing."

Ollie's expression changed from shock to confusion.

"What – get engaged? Ask her to move in with you and your dad? Get each other's names tattooed on your knees? What are you on about exactly?"

"It just came to me that I'd like to buy her a ring for her birthday next month. No, not an engagement ring. Like a... what do you call them? Like a friendship ring or something. Nothing cheap, though."

"OK, so what about going to the jewellers and asking if they do 'More-than-friendship-but-not-quite-engagement' rings? *They'd* be popular..."

"Yeah, yeah," said Matt, knowing that Ollie had slipped back very quickly into comfortable taking-the-mick mode. "But what do you think, Ol? Do you think she'd like it?"

"Maybe," shrugged Ollie. "But didn't you buy her loads for Christmas?"

Ollie was thinking of the over-the-top number of gifts his mate had bestowed upon Gabrielle – in vast contrast to the CD she'd bought Matt.

"Yeah, but I want to get her something *really* special for her birthday next month, and I think this would be great."

"Well, I s'pose... but I don't think Gaby expects loads of flash presents all the time," Ollie tried to reason. From what he and the others knew of her, Gabrielle didn't seem the type to be impressed by big gestures. "Won't she just be happy being with you?"

"I hope so," Matt grinned sheepishly. "I just want to prove to her how much I love—"

He broke off as Gabrielle waved her friend goodbye and turned to join the boys.

Ollie couldn't help but glance down at her delicate, skinny fingers and wonder what she'd make of being presented with a not-quite-engagement ring to wear on one of them...

● ● ●

"Maybe we should head off," Matt smiled at Gabrielle, keen to have her all to himself on the long, cold, romantic walk back to her house. They were sitting on a chair at the edge of the packed dance floor, Gabrielle perched on his knee.

"No, it's all right," she flicked her brown eyes fleetingly up at him, while looking on enviously at the mass of dancers in front of them. "Mum and Dad said it was OK to stay out extra late tonight as it's New Year."

Matt slid his hand under one of hers and stared down happily at it.

"But it's not like we have to stay till the very end. I've only got one box of records with me since I was using the main DJ's gear and I've locked them away in the office. I can pick them up in the week some time."

The beads in Gabrielle's hair tinkled as she turned her gaze towards him. Or at least Matt guessed they did; he couldn't make out such a delicate sound above the dance music that was blasting out.

"No," she said firmly. "I'm having a good time. I don't want to leave yet."

Matt let his fingers wrap themselves around hers and squeezed them.

"OK, whatever you want," he beamed back at her.

The pressure of his secret decision was pressing at his chest and he wasn't at all sure he could keep himself from telling her.

"I *have* made a resolution tonight, you know," he grinned, giving in.

"What's that?" she asked distractedly, once again more absorbed in the dancers than Matt.

"I decided I'm going to buy you a ring for your birthday," he said, lifting her hand to his mouth and gently kissing it.

"A ring?" she asked, flashing her brown eyes wide at him. "What kind of ring?"

"An eternity ring," he explained, pleased with himself for remembering the proper name for what he had in mind since his conversation with Ollie half an hour before.

"Eternity..." repeated Gabrielle.

"Pleased?" asked Matt, rubbing her nose affectionately with his own.

"Mmm!" Gabrielle half-nodded, giggling nervously.

"But I didn't mean to tell you – it was supposed to be a surprise," Matt confessed. "Let's talk about something else."

"What sort of something else?" asked Gabrielle, wriggling uncomfortably on his knee.

I've made a mistake telling her so soon, Matt realised. *She's gone all shy on me...*

"Well, what about resolutions – are you sure you don't have any? I mean, *I* changed my mind..."

Gabrielle bit her lip and looked away.

"What's up? Have I said something wrong?"

"Matt," she replied after a second, staring down at her hand still cradled in his. "I want to have more fun."

"Well, I guess that's a good resolution to have," he smiled.

"No, you don't understand," she said, shaking her head, but not meeting his gaze. "When I say fun, I mean, like... like *freedom*."

"Freedom?" asked Matt blankly, ducking his head down slightly to try and read her expression.

"Freedom," she repeated, a soft warm tear dropping from her eye on to the skin of his wrist.

"Which means?"

"Which means... no more me and you..."

Apart from the wetness of her tear, all Matt was aware of was a large, invisible vice closing tight around his heart as her words sank in.

CHAPTER 4

• •

A SNEAK IN THE DARK

"Well, I guess this is where we all go our separate ways," said Maya, glad of the snuggliness of her black puffa coat in the icy air.

It was late at night, or very early in the morning to be exact, and everyone was starting to flag. It had taken them forever to get ready for the walk home from the town hall – mainly because they'd wasted a long time searching for Matt, who was missing, presumed walking Gabrielle home.

Going via the park wasn't the most obvious route home for some of the crowd – Cat in particular – but it was as if they wanted to stay together, making this first night of the year last as long as possible. And now, after their stroll along the silent streets, interrupted only by the occasional passing taxi and the odd thump of music spilling from house parties along the way, they'd ended up on the pavement opposite Winstead park's east gate.

Cat, Ollie and Joe would be heading north together, with Joe and Ollie's arms coming in handy to help Cat keep her balance (frosty pavements and six-inch heels didn't really go), while Maya would be heading off home in the direction of the residential streets close to St Mark's school on the opposite side of the park.

She'd have company for a few minutes more of her walk; Anna and Owen would continue on towards the End-of-the-Line café, above which was situated Anna's tiny flat. Sonja and Kerry would be walking on with Anna and her brother as far as Station Road, where Kerry expected a lengthy stop for goodnight smooches before she could drag Sonja away from Owen and point her homewards.

But not everyone was quite ready to end the night so soon.

"Hey – how about sneaking into the park?" Ollie suddenly suggested, ignoring Maya's prelude to breaking the party up.

"What for?" asked Cat dubiously.

"Fun! Heard of it?" Ollie answered, picking Cat up in a bear hug. She started shrieking as he spun her round in a circle.

"But it's all locked up and we probably shouldn't—" Kerry protested feebly. She never felt very comfortable breaking rules, but she also knew that once Ollie got enthusiastic about something, it was pretty hard to get him to change his mind.

"Ah, come on, you lot – it's not like we're vandals or anything. It'll just be sort of magical to be in there alone. Kind of spooky and weird, like Anna's crazy staring-at-the-New-Year-sky thing."

"Thanks – you're making me sound as bonkers as Mad Vera in the launderette, Ol," laughed Anna, thinking of the old dear who regularly entertained the staff and regulars of the café. They'd watch her from across the road as she merrily waltzed her mop around the washing machines, encouraging all her customers to join in as she trilled along to the radio. Even if it was only tuned to the news. You could always tell the people who were new to the launderette: they'd be the ones looking mortified and trying to hide behind their newspapers.

"Well, at least the old girl would be more fun than *you* lot tonight – you bunch of cowards are acting more like pensioners than she ever does!"

"Ollie, can I just say something?" interrupted Sonja. "Like massively high gates and sharp, pointy railings?"

"And, can I just say, broken railing just up there?" Ollie pointed up beyond the east gate. "Which gives easy access to small boys and party animals like ourselves!"

"Is it large enough for us big boys to get through, though?" grinned Owen.

"No problemo," said Ollie matter-of-factly, grabbing Kerry by the hand and making his way across the road. "Don't know if it's big enough for Cat's head, though. Or her chest."

"You little—!" gasped Cat, teetering after Ollie and Kerry, and lashing out at his back with her handbag.

"Missed!" he cackled, breaking into a run and dragging Kerry with him. "You'll have to catch me before you can hit me!"

The other five glanced at the farcical sight of Cat clattering her way across the road in not-very-hot pursuit.

"Come on then," shrugged Sonja. "I guess we're all going to the park."

● ● ●

The faint squeak-squeak of the roundabout was the only sound they could make out. They couldn't even hear the rumble of a late-night car growling along on the nearby road: it was as if the tall trees round the edge of the park had swallowed up all the night's sounds that might intrude on their stolen time there.

"Ollie was right, this is beautiful," Anna murmured, her eyes fixed to the stars that were winking in the sky above.

"It's better if you lie down," said Joe from his reclining position.

Anna glanced around her in the dark and saw that Maya, Cat, Sonja and Owen had already copied him and lay flat on their backs on the gently turning roundabout.

"You sound like you've done this before, Joe," Anna laughed, settling herself back on her elbows.

"He has," came Maya's voice from beside her. "Me and my little brother have caught him at it. When Joe's about, none of the kids can get on their roundabout 'cause this nasty man's nicked it and is lying there daydreaming."

Joe smiled to himself, remembering the time Maya and Ravi had found him whirling round, cloud-gazing and listening on his headphones to a rough mix of the song he'd secretly written for Kerry.

"Where've Kerry and Ollie gone?" asked Cat suddenly as if she'd unconsciously tuned into Joe's thoughts.

Anna peered into the shadowy distance and saw a faint glint of Ollie's light-grey cord jacket.

"I think they're over by the fountain," she replied, squinting, before the slow spin of the roundabout changed her view.

"Huh – I bet it's getting sick-bucket slushy over there," grunted Cat. "It'll be all, 'Ooh, this is our first New Year together, baby...' Yuk!"

"Don't know why you're so cynical, Cat," came Sonja's voice, "considering that great, big, soppy resolution you came out with earlier about wanting to get married. Ha!"

Joe wasn't aware of the two cousins as they started to bicker. He'd fixed his eyes on one bright star, pressed the rewind button in his mind and was slowing reliving that kiss with Kerry...

• • •

"It is beautiful," sighed Kerry cuddling into Ollie as they sat on the edge of the Victorian granite fountain, staring out at the soft, dark stillness around them.

"See? I knew it would be a nice way to end the night, instead of us all just scurrying home."

"Mind you, I think I'd be calling it *scary*, rather than beautiful, if *you* weren't here," she smiled to herself, resting her head on his shoulder.

"That's my job! To take care of you," Ollie replied, kissing her lightly on the forehead.

Kerry felt so happy that the little niggles that had been trying to interrupt and upset her night faded away. Almost.

"It's going to be a good year, I can feel it," said Ollie, gazing up at the stars. "The band... us. What do you say, Kez?"

"Well, I hope so," she murmured, the dormant niggles and that sense of guilt for what she'd done rearing up inside her once again.

"I know what you're thinking..."

Oh no, you don't, Ollie, she said to herself.

"You think it'll all change for the crowd when you and Joe and Sonja go to university or college or whatever. But things always change and it doesn't have to be bad. We'll still be happy, even if it means me jumping on a train to come and see you every weekend!"

Kerry felt a slight wave of comfort; at least Ollie could visualise them still being together that far into the future. But Kerry couldn't be so sure that loving each other long-distance would be easy.

She thought of Sonja and Owen; she knew that for all the blissed-out moments Sonja had when they were together, there were the long separations, the waits by the phone and the instability of everything to worry her.

It wasn't what Kerry wanted; it wasn't what Kerry wanted for her and Ollie at all.

"God, what are those two like?" Ollie interrupted her thoughts as Cat and Sonja's sniping voices drifted over. "Can't they give it a rest, just for one night?"

"Ollie, they've been like this since they both learned to talk – and before that probably – so it's no big surprise. Don't let it spoil tonight."

And with that, Kerry pushed the troublesome doubts to the back of her mind and gently pulled Ollie's face towards her again.

Just as their lips were about to touch, they both drew back and blinked in surprise.

"It's snowing..." Kerry gasped, feeling the icy flutter of flakes settle on her eyelashes and lips.

But Ollie's kiss soon melted them away.

CHAPTER 5

• •

POST-PARTY BLUES

"Neeeeeeeeeeeee-*owwwwwwww*!!"

Kerry pulled the pillow over her head and willed the waves of sleep to carry her off again.

"Bchhhh-bchhh-bchhhhh!! Ker-POW!"

Some kind of intergalactic spaceship crashed outside Kerry's room, battering a dent in the door as it was shot down in flames.

"Lewis!" barked Kerry, yanking the door open and finding her brother staring up at her from the landing. "I'm trying to sleep!"

"Sorry, Kerry..." he muttered, grabbing his Star Wars Pod Racer up from the carpet.

"And what are you doing chucking your toys around like that? You'll break that spaceship thing and you've only had it a week!"

"Sorry, Kerry..."

"And if you *have* to break it, can you go and do it somewhere in the house that isn't right outside my bedroom, please?"

"Sorry, Ke—"

Kerry slammed the door harder than she meant to and instantly felt bad. Lack of sleep hadn't helped; it felt as if she'd only just lain her head down before it was daylight and the latest instalment in the battle for Naboo had started, courtesy of Lewis.

The other thing that was weighing heavily on her this morning was the fact that when she'd stumbled out of her clothes and into bed a few short hours ago, she'd noticed with a start that the plastic bag she'd shoved under her bed a few nights previously was now sticking out. Had someone been rummaging through it?

Kerry sighed deeply. It wasn't Lewis's fault she felt like she did. There was no point taking it out on him.

"Neeeeeeeeee-*yowwwwwwwwwww*!"

"Lewis, I shouldn't have—" she began, having pulled the door open again. "*Ow!*"

Her brother picked up the spacecraft that had just collided with Kerry's shin.

"Sorry, Kerry..."

• • •

"You know what you are?" Joe told his reflection in the bathroom mirror.

His reflection gazed back at him, all sleep-tousled brown hair and eyes dark-circled through lack of sleep.

"You are *weak*," he admonished himself, full of anger at his lack of willpower the night before. "You never had the guts to go after Kerry in the first place, and you don't even have the guts to give her up now. One stupid, meaningless little kiss and you're right back to square one."

Yanking the tap on, he splashed cold water on to his face in an attempt to wake up his senses.

"Come on – prove you can do something assertive for once," he snapped at his now wide-eyed, dripping reflection. "Just one little thing to show you're not a wimpy loser..."

A thought came to him and Joe turned and made his way out into the hall, pulling a clean T-shirt over his head.

He thundered down the narrow stairs of his terraced house and made a grab for the phone, punching out numbers before he lost his bottle.

"Hello?" he said nervously as a female voice answered. "It's, uh, Joe. I just wanted to say..."

He hesitated. It was going to sound corny. But he'd phoned now – there was no going back.

"...I just wanted to say Happy New Year and everything, Gillian. Is, uh, my dad there?"

After years of blind dislike, Joe had been slowly forging a relationship with his estranged dad over the last few months. It hadn't been particularly easy or comfortable for either of them – no Waltons-style hugging and "I love you, Daddy!" But, since Joe's fateful visit in the summer, when Gillian had lost the baby she and his father had been longing for, father and son had begun to build bridges between them.

And Joe knew instinctively that phoning his dad up first(ish) thing on New Year's Day would mean a lot to him.

OK, so this isn't sorting out anything about Kerry, he told himself as he waited to hear his father's voice. *But at least it's something positive...*

● ● ●

"Catrina!"

Cat groaned and stuck her head out from under the duvet. Her bedside alarm clock said eleven o'clock-ish. She was too sleepy and tired out from last night's party to make out what it said exactly.

But whatever it is, it's way too early, she

thought, pulling the duvet back over her head and retreating into sleep.

"CATRINA!"

"What?!" she asked irritably, throwing her duvet to one side and staring at her mother in the doorway.

"Did you use up all the milk last night? There was a full pint in there when I went out. And there'll be hardly any shops open today—"

"NO! I did *not* use up all the milk, last night, OK? Now, will you *please* close the door and let me sleep?"

Sylvia Osgood stood tight-lipped in her daughter's doorway, obviously going nowhere.

"Don't be ridiculous, Cat – it's half past eleven. Get up."

"Mum, I know you've forgotten what it's like to be young," griped Cat, raising herself up on to her elbows, "but I was at a party last night, if you remember. And I didn't get in till late, so I'd like to sleep some more, *if* you don't mind."

"Well, you were in and snoring by the time I came in from *my* party."

Cat was caught out. She usually took no interest at all in her mother's social life, which tended to revolve around her boring friends from the gym where she spent her life when she wasn't at work. The thought of her mum attending a party that went on later than Cat's slightly grated with her daughter.

"Where'd you go again?" Cat asked as casually as she could.

"Your friend Matt's house," said her mother, running a manicured hand through her sharply-cut hair. "His father had a New Year's party. It was quite a laugh, actually."

Cat flopped back on the bed, her interest sapping away now that she knew it was only Matt's dad's do they were talking about. She pictured Mr Ryan's thinning hair, roly-poly build and awkwardly formal manner – you'd never guess he was related to someone as undeniably handsome and laid-back as Matt.

"Didn't know you knew Matt's dad," she yawned.

"Mmm, through friends of friends," her mother half shrugged. "Anyway, can't stand here talking. Since, by some act of God, all our milk's vanished, I'd better jump in the car and see if I can find a garage or something that's open."

Cat lay still, listening to the sound of her mother grabbing the car keys off the hall table and slamming her way out of the front door. She was about to close her eyes and luxuriate in the peace when an unpleasant memory from the night before slithered into her mind.

I told them all that my dream was to get married! she recalled, wincing at her admission of the previous night. *What on earth made me say that? They're never going to stop teasing me about it now!*

Cat loved her devil-may-care, don't-mess-with-me reputation, and the idea that she might have blown it with her mates over one stupid slip worried her. Of course, it never occurred to Cat that all her friends already knew her big mouth and barbed words hid a heart of pure sludge.

But it's true – I know it's stupid, but I think I would love to get married, she sighed to herself. *And it's not just for the big white frock. Though that would be nice...*

The reason she particularly fought against the idea was her own parents' lack of success in the wedding game. Her father was long gone and (unlike Joe's dad or Matt's mum) his whereabouts were unknown.

But maybe Mum and Dad are the reason I do fancy the idea. Maybe I want to prove that it can work, she reasoned, turning over on her side with a sigh.

It was then that her eye settled on something on the floor that brought back another memory from the night before.

The empty carton of milk and the scrunched

up packet that had once contained a considerable number of Hob-Nobs were testament to the much-later-than-midnight snack she'd helped herself to when she'd crept her way back into the house in the wee, small hours.

Cat reached out one arm, shuffled the evidence under her bed, and went back to sleep.

• • •

Matt sat slouched on the black leather sofa. He didn't seem to notice that the foot he'd kicked up on to the coffee table was now lolling sideways into the remnants of a chicken leg and coleslaw. The paper plate was just one of many strewn around the living room in the wake of his father's party.

If Matt had been in any fit state, it might have occurred to him that this party of his father's – judging by the empty bottles and general debris – looked as if it had been every bit as rowdy and successful as the sort of parties Matt himself threw when his dad was out of town.

"Matt, is that you making that racket?" groaned his father, peering sleepily round the living room door.

Matt glanced down at his hands and saw that he'd been bending, crushing and generally pulverising an empty beer can without even realising it.

"That must have been a really late party you were at," said his father, striding over in his dressing gown and plonking himself wearily on a chair. "Not been in long then?"

Matt struggled to understand the point his dad was making, then followed his gaze down to the black jacket he was still wearing.

He didn't have the energy to tell his father that the party had finished hours ago. That he'd wandered the Winstead streets aimlessly for hours before coming home. That he'd been sitting – numbed – in this exact same position since dawn.

Telling him didn't matter. Nothing mattered any more to Matt. Not now Gaby had broken up with him.

CHAPTER 6

• •

PARTY PROMISES

Despite having spent the best part of New Year's Day with Owen, Sonja was back at Anna's flat early on Sunday morning. Seeing the small, folded leaflet sticking out of Owen's jeans' pocket she grabbed it. There was his train – ringed in red pen – under the Sunday service timetable. Frowning, she scoured the list of train times under the Monday section.

"Couldn't you get a train tomorrow instead?" she said, finding it hard to make sense of the jumble of figures.

"No. The boss only gave me Friday off if I promised faithfully to come in tomorrow to help prepare for this big contract coming up. And you're glad I surprised you by arriving on Friday out of the blue, aren't you?"

"Yes, but I wish you didn't have to go. I wish you could stay a day longer..." said Sonja sadly, twisting her fingers around Owen's.

"And I wish you two would save all your fond farewells till after I've left – I've only got to find my shoes and I'll be out of your way," said Anna, scampering around the flat in her hurry not to be late for her shift. She could tell from the distant clatterings and banging in the café kitchen below that this Sunday morning was going to be a busy one.

"Anna, I'm not embarrassed to say anything in front of such a cool, understanding sister as you," Owen grinned at her as she scurried past the back of the sofa.

"Yeah, I know," she replied breathlessly, bending over to check under the chest of drawers for the missing shoes. "The only trouble is that *I'm* getting embarrassed – I feel like an eavesdropper!"

"Sorry, Anna – I shouldn't have come round so early this morning," Sonja apologised to Anna's back as her friend rifled under a chair. "It's just that I don't get enough time to see this brother of yours as it is, so I wanted to make the most of the last little while we had before he caught his train."

"Don't be silly," Anna smiled kindly, now facing the two lovebirds on her sofa and pulling on her shoes at last. "Look, that's me ready — my humble home is all yours!"

Scrambling to her feet, Anna bent over to give Owen a goodbye kiss, wished him a safe journey and flew out of the door.

"Listen, I've got something to ask you," said Owen with a certain amount of urgency in his voice as soon as Anna's footsteps could be heard stamping down the stairs outside.

Sonja's heart leapt into her throat. What was he going to say? What could have made his smile fade so quickly into seriousness?

"Can you do something for me? Well, it's for Anna, really..."

Sonja relaxed and began breathing again. So this obviously wasn't a 'Do you love me? 'Cause I love you' kind of conversation. Not yet, at least.

"Sure!" she answered him, trying to sound normal. "What's up?"

"Well, I don't know if she's said anything to you, but it's her birthday a week tomorrow."

"No, she hasn't mentioned it." Sonja shook her head in surprise. In their crowd, birthdays were quite a big thing; well, it was always a good excuse to have a night out. "I wonder why she's kept it so quiet?"

"Anna's funny that way — doesn't really like

drawing attention to herself," Owen replied with a shrug.

Sonja knew that for sure. Anna had been at the End for months before they'd all got to know her properly – even Ollie who worked with her.

Anna's reluctance to get friendly with anyone for so long had sometimes puzzled Sonja. She couldn't help thinking how lonely she must have been – a newcomer to town, hidden away in her funny little flat when she wasn't slaving away for Nick in his café.

"But what I was thinking was, it would be so nice if you and the others could do something for her."

"What? Like a surprise party?"

"Oh, I don't know – it's a Monday night after all, and that's not too inspiring. But I'd hate to think of Anna's birthday slipping by unnoticed, with her just sitting up here on her own after finishing her shift."

Sonja loved a challenge – and since Owen was doing the asking, there wasn't much chance of her refusing.

"No problem. I'll talk to everyone and see what we can come up with."

"Thanks, Son," he smiled, giving her a peck on the nose. "I just think Anna needs a bit of spoiling, since she's never had an easy time of it."

"How do you mean?" Sonja asked, noticing how flustered Owen looked immediately after the words had left his mouth.

"Oh, uh, nothing, really," he tried to laugh. "Just the way she's had to be responsible and look after herself this past year or two."

"Yeah, but she didn't have to, did she?" quizzed Sonja, sure that she wasn't misinterpreting his uneasiness. "I mean, she didn't have to leave home so young and cope on her own – that was *her* choice, wasn't it?"

Something in Owen's expression told Sonja that there might be more to it than that...

"Hey, what are we wasting time talking about my sister for when I have to leave in..." Owen looked hastily at his watch "...a quarter of an hour? C'mere, you..."

Sonja felt her curiosity fade away as soon as she was in Owen's arms.

CHAPTER 7

• •

TEA AND SYMPATHY

Anna smiled to herself as she walked into the steamy café kitchen. It was great to see Owen looking so happy; a lot of the time he took life so seriously, like getting all wrapped up in his university course, or now, in his work as a web designer.

He'd always been like that. As a little girl, Anna could remember watching Owen studiously reading the instruction notes to all the games and construction toys he'd get as presents. Most other kids would have just chucked those aside and got on with playing. But not Owen; he was too meticulous for that.

That's why Sonja and her boundless enthusiasm did him good, bringing out the sillier, more fun-loving side to him.

I've got a good feeling about those two, Anna thought to herself, letting her intuition guide her more than her head.

If she listened to what was going on up there, she'd have had serious doubts about her brother and her friend's future together: Owen lived so far away and Sonja was going to head off to university God-knows-where later on in the year. But Anna knew that when it came to tuning into people and situations, there were plenty of other senses to listen to as well as just plain common sense.

"Anna! Where've you been? It's been mad the last hour!" Nick bellowed over his shoulder, amid steam from copious pots and the sizzle of frying bacon filling the air.

"Nick, you told me not to come in till eleven o'clock today, remember? You thought it would be a slow start with everyone still recovering from the New Year," said Anna matter-of-factly, refusing to let her boss's forgetfulness rile her while she was feeling so cheery.

"Did I?" he replied, furrowing his brow and holding a spatula in the air as he racked his obviously addled brain.

"Maybe *you're* the one who still needs to recover from New Year celebrations. Were you out again last night?" Anna asked, tying on her white apron.

"Mmm," muttered Nick non-committally, turning back to his bacon.

"Anyway, if you wanted me to come in earlier, you only had to ask. I'm not exactly hard to find, am I?"

"Oh, ignore him – you know he just likes a moan," said a bright voice.

Irene, one of the two ex-dinner ladies who helped out at the End, came bustling through with a tray piled high with the remains of someone's breakfast.

"Don't I know it!" Anna agreed as she picked up her orders notepad and pen from a shelf by the door.

"Good to know my staff respect me..." said Nick huffily.

"Here," said Irene, pulling out a packet of aspirin from her pocket and slapping it on the counter beside Nick. "That should help improve your mood."

With that, she turned to Anna, winked conspiratorially and mouthed, "Too much to drink!" Anna winked back.

Nick was a little overly fond of his beer; his ample stomach would put a pot-bellied pig to shame – and at this time of year, it was no great surprise that he'd overdone it a bit.

Just as Anna was going through to the café,

she heard a terrible clatter of dishes and cutlery being loudly dumped on to the top of the dishwasher, followed by a loud groan. Irene was obviously enjoying seeing Nick suffer.

Anna wasn't as busy as she had thought she was going to be. The tables were all full, but everyone had been served and were busy eating, chatting or lazily scanning the Sunday papers. At that moment, there wasn't even any clearing up to be done – Irene had taken care of the last batch – and Anna was just about to see if she'd be more use through the back, tidying up or something, when she suddenly noticed Matt sitting, head down, at the small table by the jukebox.

Anna hadn't spotted him during her first glance around the room; Matt, Joe and the others were usually only ever to be found in their favourite spot – the roomy booth in the bay window. But today, that pride of place had gone to a noisy bunch of girls, one of whom, Anna noticed, was Maya's younger sister, Sunita.

That's not going to go down well with Maya and everyone if they're thinking of coming down today, she mused.

Anna hesitated for a second, swaying slightly as she decided what to do. She could just follow her first instinct and go back into the kitchen: Matt hadn't noticed her yet and, by the time she came back out, Sonja might be there, which would deflect any awkwardness.

But that was just stupid, she knew. Like the way she and Matt had reacted towards each other on Friday night, doing their best not to catch each other's eyes.

Come on, Anna, she told herself, directing her footsteps towards her friend. *You're nearly nineteen; you're a big girl now. Just go and talk to Matt and get over this stupid embarrassment.*

"Matt, how are you doing?" she said brightly, resting her hand on his shoulder.

She felt a jolt when he raised his face to her. His face was grey-pale, his eyes rimmed with dark shadows. Either he was sick – or something bad had happened.

"God, Matt – what's wrong?" she asked, crouching down beside him, all thought of customers and her own unease with him gone in an instant.

Matt made a snorting noise and his lips wavered at the corners. Anna suspected it was supposed to be a laugh, but you could get done by the Trades Descriptions Act for trying to pass anything so miserable off as humour.

"Nothing serious," he said, twirling the salt cellar round and round agitatedly. "I got chucked, didn't I?"

"Gabrielle *finished* with you?" asked Anna in surprise. She hadn't seen that one coming at all.

Unless you count what happened between us, she chided herself.

"Oh, yes," Matt nodded slowly. "She finished with me."

"When?"

"New Year. Not long after midnight."

"What – after we'd all been out on the fire escape together?"

"Uh-huh. Nice timing, wasn't it?" he muttered, trying for the ironic smile once again but failing miserably.

"We couldn't find you when we were leaving..." said Anna, remembering how they'd all thought it was because Matt and Gaby had disappeared off on their own for romantic reasons. How wrong could they be.

"Yeah, well, after the bombshell, there wasn't a lot of point hanging about. I phoned a taxi and dropped her off. Ha! That was one silent journey..."

The tinkle of the bell above the café alerted Anna to the fact that she had a job to do, but she didn't want to leave Matt in the middle of his confessional. Luckily, Irene, who'd just come back through from the kitchen, must have instantly read the signs; she made a motion for Anna to stay where she was while she trotted over to see to the newly arrived customers.

"But why, Matt? What reason did she have to finish with you?"

"I'm too serious, apparently," he practically spat out. "I make her feel too claustrophobic. She just wants 'a laugh' and to 'have fun', and she doesn't get any of that with me."

"Oh, Matt," said Anna, making a grab for his hand – partly for comfort and partly to stop him making that racket with the salt cellar.

Suddenly, it all made a little more sense to her. On Christmas night, when Matt had come back to her flat, Anna had been taken aback when she heard how many presents he'd bought Gabrielle and how much money he'd blown on her. It had seemed a bit over-the-top, but Anna hadn't said anything.

Poor Gaby – she must have been feeling steamrollered by Matt, thought Anna, without realising how far her friend had been willing to go to prove his affection. His next words confirmed her thoughts.

"I wish I hadn't told her about the ring – it was like that made up her mind," groaned Matt. "Why couldn't I just keep my big mouth shut?"

"Ring?" said Anna a little too loudly, shock getting the better of her. She quickly lowered her voice before she spoke again. "What ring, Matt?"

"I told her I wanted to get her an eternity ring for her birthday," he answered bleakly. "I can't believe it – this is the first girl I treat with any respect and she tells me I'm boring!"

Anna squeezed his hand and bit her tongue for a moment. It seemed that Matt had gone from one extreme to the other – from heartless flirt to Total Commitment Man – without realising there was plenty of scope in between.

Gaby must have been expecting him to come out with stuff about 2.4 children and what shrubs they should buy for their future garden together, Anna thought. *And all the girl wanted was a bit of romance and a nice guy to have a laugh with. Poor Gaby – and poor Matt!*

"Course, I can't help feeling that wasn't the real reason she chucked me," mumbled Matt, glancing up cagily at Anna.

"What're you on about?" she asked.

Fleetingly, she wondered if the subject of sex had anything to do with it. At eighteen, Matt was four years older than Gabrielle, so for all Anna knew, there was a possibility it had caused problems. And everyone knew what a rampaging babe-hunter he'd been before he met Gaby. But then again, she reasoned, Matt was so crazy about Gaby that there didn't seem much chance that he'd do anything to mess things up between them.

"I can't help thinking that somehow Gaby found out," he shrugged.

"Found out what?"

"About you and me..." Matt answered, fixing his eyes on hers. "About what happened Christmas night."

CHAPTER 8

• •

ANNA, MATT AND ONE STUPID MISTAKE

"What do you mean, what happened on Christmas night?" Anna glared at him, struggling to keep her voice down. "Matt, it was silly, it was stupid, and I know we've both been avoiding talking about it, but you can't use that as a reason for Gaby finishing with you!"

"But what if she did somehow find out?" he whimpered, fixing pathetic, puppy-dog eyes on her.

"Like how?" Anna tried to reason. "Did you tell anyone? 'Cause I certainly didn't!"

"No, I didn't say a word—"

"Well then," she interrupted him, "are you trying to say that she employed a private eye to trail us after we left the park together? Maybe he climbed up a ladder and took photos of us through my front window!"

"Aw, listen, I know it sounds crazy," Matt said almost apologetically. "It's just that I can't get my head around anything at the moment."

"Matt, you're *allowed* to feel awful about breaking up with Gaby – you wouldn't be human if you didn't," said Anna, more gently. "But don't go looking for conspiracy theories. You and me, we were both in the same boat that afternoon; both feeling a bit lonely, being the only two not doing the big, happy, family thing at Christmas. We were feeling sorry for ourselves and we got carried away with the emotion of it all."

"But we shouldn't have—"

"No, we shouldn't have," she shushed him, putting a finger up to his lips. That one small gesture triggered a memory of what they felt like pressed against her own lips. "Matt, we can't change anything. We kissed – that's all. Don't give yourself a hard time about it."

"I can't help—"

"Sorry," smiled Irene apologetically, leaning over them at the small table. "A few customers need their bills now, Anna. Can you give me a hand?"

"Oh, Irene, of course. Thanks for letting us have a bit of time," said the waitress, scrambling to her feet. "Are you going to be OK, Matt?"

Matt nodded and gave her a weak smile.

"Sure," he said, dropping his gaze to the table as soon as she stepped away.

"Better shove another coffee under your friend's nose," Irene whispered to Anna. "You know what Nick's like – if he looks out here and sees the lad doing nothing more than moping at a table that could have paying customers on it, he'll just start griping!"

Anna knew Irene was right. Nick was matey enough with Matt – as he was with nearly all Ollie's friends (Cat excepted, thanks to past misdeeds), but when it came to matters of money, that was something different entirely.

She was just sliding a cup under the cappuccino machine with one hand while adding up a customer bill with the other, when a voice suddenly disturbed her juggling act.

"Hi there," said Rudi, one of the two Dutch boys who had become regulars at the End.

"Hi," smiled Anna, feeling slightly frazzled. "Take a seat, Rudi – I'll get your order in a second."

"No – I only need to ask, will your friend Cat be here this morning?" he asked, in slightly faltering English.

"Don't know, to be honest. Why don't you ask Matt over there?" she said, indicating with a nod to where Matt was slouching. "And here, do me a favour and give him this while you're at it."

Rudi took the coffee cup and saucer from her and, with a grin, turned and made his way over to Matt.

"For you, from your waitress friend," he announced, putting the steaming coffee in front of Matt. "And I have a question for you."

"Oh, yeah?" said Matt, disinterestedly. "What's that then?"

"Your friend Cat. Is she coming here today? Or do you know how I can speak with her?"

Matt furrowed his brow as he tried to sort out his messed-up mind. He didn't know if Cat was coming, but he had her phone number, and those of all his other friends, programmed into his mobile. He patted at the empty pockets of his jacket and realised that in his present disorganised state, he'd left it at home.

"Um, her number... it's, uh... no, it's... God, I can't remember." He shook his head, his brain too frazzled to think straight. Then without thinking, he reeled off her address.

"Thank you," said Rudi, heading off towards the door. "I'll see you on Thursday, maybe? When the group play – OK?"

"Yeah, sure, whatever," Matt replied.

He suddenly thought of Cat and the others, and realised he didn't have the energy to go through his whole shabby story again; not after spilling it all to Anna. He stood up, glanced round for Anna and, seeing no sign of her, left, before any of his friends had the chance to catch him.

Anna, who'd been down behind the counter fetching a bottle of ketchup, straightened up and immediately spotted the empty table by the jukebox, a cup of cappuccino still steaming on it.

"Thanks, Matt," she muttered to herself, grabbing a handful of coins from her tips jar and dropping them into the till to pay for what her absent-minded friend hadn't.

CHAPTER 9

• •

IT'S ALL IN THE MIND

Joe moved his fingers one by one in his jacket pockets, mentally counting off the points on his list. He'd only made up the list the night before, lying awake for hours, running through it in his head, finalising it all even as sleep eventually slipped over him.

Now, stomping along past the park towards the End, he was already on the third run-through since he'd left his house, and was only dimly aware of the Sunday morning shrieking coming from the children's playground on the other side of the railings.

Normally, he enjoyed watching the kids running around as he passed by; he liked the way they seemed so happy, carefree and unconcerned by stuff that bothered him – like A levels, college choices and unrequited love for his best friend's girlfriend...

Which was what the list was all about: Ten Ways To Forget About Kerry. Just vaguely *wanting* to get over her wasn't enough, he'd realised after his New Year relapse. He had to be more scientific about it, work on it as if he was studying for an exam – come up with all those little sentences or rhymes that were meant to help you remember dates and formulas.

Joe touched his pinky finger as he reached number ten and then felt an instant compunction to run through the whole list again.

1. *Stop thinking of Kerry as perfect – she's got faults just like everyone else,* he recited silently to himself, immediately picturing how her nose crinkled cutely when she giggled and how beautiful the flecks of gold were in her hazel eyes, especially when they were accentuated by her little wire-rimmed specs.

2. *Realise that the longer this goes on, the more chance Kerry has of finding out my true feelings, and she'd be mortified – it could ruin the friendship we've already got.*

3. *When I catch myself dreaming about her, I must force myself to think of something else straightaway.*

4. *Remind myself that loving someone secretly*

hurts too much and I deserve to be happy as much as anyone.

5. Stop looking for hidden meanings in every look or word from Kerry – she's only reacting the way she would to any of the others.

6. Be aware that being in love with Kerry is a total betrayal of my best mate – and Ollie doesn't deserve that.

7. Keep remembering that the real love of my life could be passing me by, all because I'm so wrapped up in this obsession for Kerry.

8. Try not to be in her company too much, while I'm trying to wean myself off her for good.

9. Stop writing songs that are basically all about Kerry.

"Hi!" A voice interrupted his recitation.

Joe felt irked. He still had another point to add. Number ten – the fact that he had to accept that Kerry didn't love him back and he had no reason to expect that she ever would.

"Hi," replied Joe, finding his path barred by one of the two Dutch lads who had been tagging along with the band or trailing after Cat. Joe couldn't be too sure that Cat's charms weren't more interesting than The Loud's songs of a Thursday night in the Railway Tavern.

"Going to the café?" asked Rudi.

"Uh, yeah," nodded Joe. Something about Rudi that morning struck him as being slightly odd, but he was too preoccupied with his list to work out what it was.

"I've just been there. Today, it's very busy."

"Did you see any of my crowd down there?" asked Joe, wondering if he'd be first or last to arrive for the ritual Sunday morning gathering.

"The tall guy with the dark hair – Matt. But he left when I did."

Fleetingly, Joe puzzled over that. Why would Matt just up and leave before anyone else arrived?

The two boys stood shuffling in silence for half a second. It was one thing to chat when there were a whole heap of people around, but one-on-one, Rudi and Joe didn't have an awful lot to say to one another.

"Uh, where are you off to then?" said Joe, all of a sudden realising what was odd about the guy in front of him: the fact that he was on his own. Since Rudi and Marc had landed in Winstead (taking a break from their round-the-world travels before returning back home to Holland) Joe had never seen one out without the other.

"Um, I just have to go see someone," muttered Rudi vaguely. "I'd better go. Bye!"

"Bye..." said Joe as Rudi hurried off.

The Dutch lad out without his sidekick and

being mysterious; Matt disappearing off on his own...

What a funny start to the day, thought Joe, starting to count through his list again as he carried on walking.

• • •

Matt Damon gave her an impish grin, ran a hand through his mop of thick blond hair and said, "Listen, there's something I've been meaning to ask you..."

She held her breath and watched as he fumbled in his pocket. Her heart leapt into her mouth when she saw the antique ring that he held out to her, dangling it on a piece of red ribbon.

"Will you marry me, Cat?"

"Oh, Matt!" she gasped, "I—"

"Catrina! You're not even dressed yet!"

Looking up from her copy of *OK!*, Cat left her fantasy behind and yawned.

"So what?" she shrugged, feeling perfectly comfortable in her fluffy dressing gown and with her feet perched up on the kitchen table.

"Because we're going to your Uncle Tom and Aunt Helena's for lunch today, remember?" said her mother irritably, shaking her hands to dry her newly varnished nails.

"*Booooo*-ring," mumbled Cat in a flat-toned grumble that was worthy of a sulky nine-year-old.

"You know something, Catrina? I could happily throttle you sometimes. Just be glad that I've only just done my nails and don't particularly want to smudge them."

"Love you too, Mommy," said Cat sarcastically under her breath as her mother flounced off.

She looked back down to the copy of *OK!* that was balanced on her knees and sighed as her eyes fixed once more on the photos of Hollywood's glitterati at some ultra-glam party. And there was Matt Damon grinning out at her cheekily again, his arm around his buddy Ben Affleck.

"Ben Affleck..." muttered Cat dreamily.

Ben Affleck gave her a devilish smile, ran a hand through his cropped dark hair and said, "Listen, there's something I've been meaning to ask you..."

She held her breath and watched as he fumbled in his pocket. Her heart leapt into her mouth when she saw the antique ring that he held out to her, dangling it on a piece of red ribbon.

"Will you marry me, Cat?"

"Oh, Ben!" she gasped, "I—"

"The door!" she heard her mother yelling above the persistent brrrr-ing of the bell. "*Catrina!* Are you deaf? Answer the door!"

Cat sighed and slapped the magazine on the table. Pulling the towelling belt of her dressing gown tighter, she stomped along the hallway, throwing a dirty look at the closed bathroom door, a look aimed at the woman behind it.

That was the trouble: spending a Sunday afternoon at Sonja's wasn't what bothered her – she liked her cousin's parents a lot. But having to spend enforced family time with her mum didn't exactly fill Cat with joy.

"Oh... hello!" said Cat, genuinely surprised to find Rudi on her doorstep.

"I'm sorry to be disturbing you," he muttered apologetically, pointing vaguely at her dressing gown and looking slightly sheepish.

"No problem," replied Cat, instantly glad that she'd followed her normal ritual of slapping on a bit of mascara the instant she woke up. She'd pulled her hair up into a topknot when she was waiting for her toast earlier and could feel loose tendrils from it curling around her neck and face. She hoped the effect was messily sexy.

"I'm shy to say this," he smiled at her, his English slipping due to his obvious nervousness, "but I have a question I must ask of you."

Cat felt a jolt as the coincidence hit her. She'd been playing with questions in her head all morning so far. In fact, before she'd been inspired by the glossy party pictures of Matt 'n' Ben, she'd even run through her favourite fantasy with Rudi's friend Marc doing the dangling ring trick.

How weird that Rudi's turned up with a question now, she thought to herself. *And it's funny how it's him and not Marc. Maybe I've been fooling around with the wrong boy...*

Like Marc, Rudi had a nice tan and golden highlighted hair from his travels to the beaches of Thailand and Australia.

Marc's better looking, she mused, *but Rudi's cute too – got that sweet little gap between his front teeth...*

"May I ask it?" he smiled uncertainly.

"Oh, yes, sure," said Cat, trying to focus her thoughts. "I'm sorry I can't ask you in, though, my mum's kind of *on* one."

Rudi looked a little confused.

"Having a rant," Cat tried to explain. "In a bad mood."

"Ah," nodded Rudi. "Well, my question is..."

Cat tossed her hair a little, feeling the dressing gown slip sexily off one shoulder.

"Yes?" she purred, waiting to be asked out.

...she watched as he fumbled in his pocket. Her heart leapt into her mouth when she saw the antique ring that Rudi held out to her, dangling it on a piece of red ribbon...

"Cat, I'm crazy about your friend Maya. Do you think I would have a chance if I asked her out?"

Cat yanked her dressing gown back on to her shoulder and sighed.

CHAPTER 10

● ●

TABLE FOR TWO

Kerry had got out of the house by the skin of her teeth.

Her dad looked up from his Sunday paper and made some comment about the article he'd just read about student fees. That was when Kerry knew she was in trouble; either he or her mum was about to launch into some big chat about life and college and everything. Just exactly what Kerry *didn't* want to talk about.

Her parents had been skirting round the subject for a while now. Not in a serious, your-future-depends-on-it! way, like Maya had to put up with from her super-ambitious parents, but they obviously felt they had to show an interest.

With her mind whirring, Kerry nearly bashed into two young girls, who'd tumbled out of a newsagent, pulling open the bags of crisps they'd just bought.

Wow, I remember being that young, she smiled to herself, steering her way past them. *All I used to stress out about in those days was what flavour Monster Munch to get and if boys could see the reflection of my pants if my school shoes were too shiny. And look at me now. Why can't everything stay the same? When did everything get so complicated?*

Things were about to get more complicated: walking past the bay window of the End, she saw with a certain amount of surprise that the booth she and her friends usually laid claim to was already taken; by Maya's little sister, of all people.

She glanced at her watch – how late was it?

Where are the others? she wondered, pushing the door open. *Usually someone makes it down early enough to snaffle our table...*

Of the others, the only ones Kerry could make out in the crowded room were Anna, rushing around with her order pad in hand, and Joe, uncomfortably sharing a table for four with a couple of old dears.

"Hi, Kerry!" he waved at her.

Kerry smiled as she saw the red flush spread over his face.

He still hasn't got over that habit of blushing

when he first sees any of us girls, she thought to herself.

"Well, at least we've got each other for company, Joe," she grinned, pulling out the seat opposite him. "I thought no one else was here when I looked through the window!"

Bang goes point number eight on my list, thought Joe, glad to see her – for all his resolve to try not to be in her company so much.

"Just as well there's only the two of us, since there's no other seats left anyway," said Joe.

"God – I'd completely forgotten; Sonja said she wouldn't be in today anyway," Kerry remembered aloud. "She's seeing Owen off on his train, then her folks are having family round for Sunday lunch – so that's Cat out too."

"Ollie not coming?" Joe asked.

"He would have done – it's his day off," said Kerry, taking her glasses off and rubbing the steaminess off them. "But he's helping his parents out at the pub today; they're short-staffed; a couple of people are off with flu."

"Maya's feeling a bit fluey too – Sunny told me when I came in," Joe indicated the giggling group of girls in the window.

He was blushing again, Kerry noticed – probably at the memory of being cackled at by Maya's sister and her cronies. Sunny was a bit of a sly minx and Kerry inwardly bet she'd made some snidey comment about Joe the minute his back was turned.

"And Matt was in earlier, but left," Joe added, checking off the roll call of their mates.

"Did he? Why didn't he stick around...?"

"Speaking about Matt?" interrupted Anna as she scurried past. "I've got something to tell you. I'll be back right after I sort these people out."

"Sounds intriguing..." said Kerry, widening her eyes.

Joe was suddenly aware that he was staring into them.

"You– you're wearing your specs a lot again," he wittered, hoping he'd covered himself.

"Yeah, I wear my contacts too, but I still find it such a hassle putting them in," Kerry explained, thinking that everything in her life was a bit of a hassle. "I don't think I'll ever be completely relaxed about sticking those bits of plastic on my eyeballs!"

Joe smiled. Kerry liked it when he gave one of those big, unself-conscious smiles – it was lovely to see him lose that haunted look he wore a lot of the time, even for a little while.

Honestly, he takes life even more seriously than me, she thought to herself.

"Here I am," said Anna, squatting down on

her knees to their level. "I can't stop, so I'll make it quick – Matt's in a mess. Gaby finished with him at New Year."

"No!" gasped Kerry in unison with Joe. She hated to hear about people breaking up: it cast a shadow over her own happiness with Ollie. "What happened?"

"I'll tell you later," Anna said quietly, indicating that their conversation was being listened in to.

The two old ladies sharing the table coughed a little, resuming their conversation as if they hadn't been earwigging like crazy.

"And he'll tell you himself, I'm sure," she continued. "I just thought you'd better know so you could be a bit sympathetic next time you speak to him."

"Yeah, thanks, Anna. We'll pass that on so no one puts their foot in it and says something tactless," said Kerry, immediately thinking, like the other two, of Cat.

"And I'll phone him later," Joe nodded, feeling terrible for Matt but at the same time wondering what he could possibly say that would help him out at a time like this.

"Good," smiled Anna, straightening up and getting back to work.

Still conscious that their conversation was being monitored, Kerry and Joe kept their comments on the situation to a minimum. Having two nosy strangers know about their friend's misery didn't seem fair.

"He hadn't told Ollie then?" said Joe in a low voice, aware that Matt was closer to Ollie than to himself.

"Nope – Ollie would've said," Kerry replied, leaning her elbow on the table and holding her hand up to cover one side of her mouth from prying eyes.

"Not good news..." Joe mused.

"So much for the start of the year – there's *no* good news," said Kerry flatly thinking more especially of her own problems than Matt's.

"Well, I've got one bit of *semi*-decent piece of news, if you can call it that," shrugged Joe. "I told my dad on the phone yesterday that my resolution was to learn to drive but that I was too skint to do it, and he said he'd give me lessons."

"Joe, that's brilliant!"

Kerry was genuinely thrilled for him; not just because it meant he could fulfil his wish, but it meant that Joe and his dad would have the chance to get closer. She was sure a lot of Joe's anxiety was to do with the break-up of his parents: she just didn't realise that another chunk of it had plenty to do with her...

"I'm going out to see him tomorrow to talk about it."

"A day out in the country..." said Kerry dreamily, imagining the picturesque village Joe's dad and girlfriend lived in. "I'm jealous – me and Ollie were going to go out on the Vespa tomorrow since the weather's supposed to be pretty clear."

"What – and now he's got to help out at The Swan?"

"Well, that, yes," she laughed with a tinge of irony, "*and* the fact that the Vespa's packed up again!"

"Again? What's fallen off it now?" Joe was laughing back.

"Ooh, I think he said it was the propeller shaft..." said Kerry, crinkling up her nose as she tried to remember.

"Kerry, it's a moped, not a plane!"

They both started sniggering so hard that the old ladies began to tut.

"Hey," said Joe as they got their breath back, "if you still fancy a day out in the country tomorrow, why don't you come along with me?"

As soon as the words were out of his mouth, Joe felt dizzy.

That was a stupid idea, he told himself off, *considering the list I wasted my time coming up with, and the fact that she's going to say no.*

Kerry hesitated for a second. The idea of just the two of them going off together was strange somehow.

But if I stay at home, there's more chance of Mum and Dad hassling me, she thought, knowing that they'd both still be off work and liable to want to 'chat'.

"Sure," she smiled shyly at Joe. "I'd love that."

CHAPTER 11

• •

IN THE LINE OF FIRE

"You're so lucky to have children with brains, Tom," said Cat's mother, blowing a funnel of smoke over the dining table.

Sonja glanced over at Cat, who rolled her eyes wearily, knowing the dig was at her expense. Sonja threw her next glance at her father – he seemed to be struggling to find the right thing to say. Holding his own when it came to work was one thing, but dealing with his razor-tongued sister was another.

"But, Sylvia, you're so lucky that Catrina knew what she wanted to do," Sonja's mother spoke instead, pushing the apple crumble she hadn't finished to one side, annoyed that Cat's mum had so insensitively lit up a cigarette. "OK, so Sonja's got her mind set on PR and Karin was very sure about her languages, but Peter had to swap courses in his first year at university when he realised he'd made a mistake, and Lottie dropped out of her course when she got the chance of a job."

"Yes, Helena, but doing some stupid Beauty Therapy course at college when she could have gone to university – can you see the sense in that?" Sylvia Osgood snorted.

Cat's mum had all but given up hassling her daughter about that snap decision to drop out of sixth form back in September. But today's Sunday lunch with her brother's family was the perfect excuse to give vent to her feelings again.

"There's nothing wrong with a course like that – there's a lot of opportunity nowadays with the health and fitness boom," Helena Harvey continued, shooting a comforting smile at her niece. "Anyway, Sylvia, I don't see the point in looking down on technical colleges. They often teach subjects that are a lot more relevant to the real world than some of the weird and wonderful ones you get at university."

Sonja felt a surge of pride for her mother; not just for standing up to Cat's mum, but for her complete lack of snobbery, despite the fact that the Harveys had all the trappings of a more than comfortable middle-class life.

Then again, as her parents had explained to her, her Aunt Sylvia had a real chip on her shoulder after being deserted by her husband, bringing up a daughter alone, putting herself through university and eventually making a success of her career.

Still doesn't give her the right to be such a bitch... thought Sonja, glaring over at her aunt.

"Anyway, how's that bloke at your work? Still giving you trouble?" Sonja's dad interjected, trying in his own way to help by getting his sister off the subject of Catrina and all her supposed failings.

Like everyone in the Harvey household, he had a soft spot for Cat, even though they knew how whiny and demanding she could be. She'd practically lived at their house for chunks of her childhood while Sylvia struggled to get on her feet.

"Sonja, Catrina – could you be loves and clear all the dishes through to the kitchen?"

"Sure, Mum," Sonja smiled at her mother, knowing that it was her way of getting the girls – Cat in particular – out of Sylvia's line of fire.

As she picked up the crockery nearest her, she saw a blur of Cat and plates already speeding out the door.

• • •

"You know what I said at New Year? My resolution, I mean?" said Cat, staring at the dial on the dishwasher and trying to decipher its code.

"What, about wanting to get married?" laughed Sonja, wiping her hands with a towel.

"Yeah, well that was just a moment of madness. My *real* resolution is to get your parents to adopt me."

"Cat, I think you're a bit too old to adopt at seventeen."

"Well, I better stick to my original plan and get married then. Find myself a young, handsome Lottery winner with a flash house, who'll take me away from my darling mother."

Cat did a quick eeny-meeny-miny-mo and spun the dial round to a random number, mentally hoping it would be OK. At least it couldn't shrink dishes, as she regularly did at home with clothes in the dryer.

"I know your mum's being a pain today, but she's not like that *all* the time," Sonja tried to pacify her, although she doubted it was true.

"Oh, come on, Son – why do you think your sisters scarpered before pudding?" said Cat, straightening up and resting her bottom against a kitchen unit. "They weren't meeting any friends – they just wanted to get away from my mother's sniping as soon as they could..."

"I think it's more the fact that they can't keep a straight face when they see your mum these days – not since I told them about her big love affair with Nick!"

Both girls broke into giggles and had to shush each other in case they attracted attention from the other room. But they found it hard to let up: the combination of Cat's mum (all corporate efficiency and gym-toned body) and Ollie's Uncle Nick ('70s throwback with a beer belly) was as unlikely a duo as Madonna and a Teletubby.

"Anyway, my mother's not the only one giving me grief today," said Cat, once they'd got their sniggers under control.

"Why? Who else is doing your head in?" asked Sonja, pouring them both some juice from the fridge.

"I got a visit today from a certain Dutch lad..."

"What – Marc came up to your flat? I didn't know you'd given him your address."

"I didn't – and it wasn't Marc. It was Rudi."

"I see you haven't lost your touch for getting into messes," Sonja teased. "Are they fighting for your attentions now, Ms Osgood?"

"I wish! And *you* can talk, Son, considering you two-timed your precious Owen when you were first seeing him."

Sonja stuck out her lip and gave a little shrug.

She hated to be reminded of doing the dirty on Owen, but she tried to reason that it was before she realised just how strongly she felt about him. It had taken a couple of dates with a ratbag like Kyle for her to come to her senses.

"So what *did* Rudi want?" Sonja asked, without responding to her cousin's jibe.

"My help in getting him a date with Maya!"

"Really?" gasped Sonja at this great bit of gossip. "I didn't realise he had a thing for her!"

"Poor bloke," sniffed Cat. "He doesn't realise he's fallen for the fussiest girl in Winstead. If Billy isn't good enough for her, then Rudi's got no chance."

"Cat, just 'cause Maya didn't fancy Billy when he was keen on her doesn't make her fussy."

Sonja was feeling a little uncomfortable with the way the conversation was going. Billy – Maya's friend from her photography club and now guitarist for The Loud – had once told Sonja in confidence that he was still crazy about Maya. She knew she shouldn't have, but Sonja couldn't stop herself from telling Kerry what he'd said; she sure wasn't going to let anything spill to Cat, who'd open her mouth and broadcast it to the world in a heartbeat.

"Listen, Owen told me something this morning," said Sonja, changing the subject as quickly as her father had done earlier at the table. "It's Anna's birthday a week tomorrow. He asked if we could maybe do something nice for her."

"God – bummer timing for a birthday," Cat replied unenthusiastically. "Right after Christmas and New Year, when everyone's partied out and broke. And it's a Monday."

"I know. And she's working. Not a lot of scope for making it a happening event, is there?" said Sonja. "But we should still try and come up with something nice."

"Yep – Anna's worth it. I haven't a clue what, though, have you?"

"Nope. We'll just have to ask the others and see if anyone comes up with anything."

"What about Kerry? She's into all this party organising thing. She did one for her brother a couple of months ago..."

"She only helped out; she didn't organise it. And anyway, Cat," said Sonja, fixing her cousin with a pale blue-eyed stare, "there's a bit of difference between throwing a party for a seven-year-old boy and putting together some kind of birthday surprise for a nineteen-year-old girl!"

"Dunno," said Cat dreamily. "Some of those kids' games look fun. We could play musical chairs in the caff and I could end up collapsing in the lap of some visiting handsome young Lottery winner, who'd just popped in for a doughnut and a cup of tea..."

"Yeah, *sure*," grinned Sonja.

"Anyway, speaking of Kerry," said Cat, "do you think she's all right? She's gone kind of quiet on me lately..."

"Probably 'cause she can't get a word in edgeways," joked Sonja. But she felt herself that Kerry was holding something back. Kerry never could hide her thoughts; her big hazel eyes registered worry without her even realising.

"Aw, you know what I mean," said Cat, pulling a face at her.

"Well, I think Kez has just got herself in a bit of a state about where to go when it comes to university, and if she really wants to be a primary teacher like she decided."

"What's she been saying about it?"

"Nothing – that's the problem. Whenever I've brought up the subject, she just clams up. Which is why I think it's that that's bothering her."

Sonja tutted and stared down at the floor.

"What's wrong?" asked Cat, immediately concerned.

"Oh, I just felt guilty all of a sudden. I'm supposed to be her best mate and with everything being so busy lately..."

"And with Owen turning up," Cat added.

"And with Owen turning up," Sonja nodded, "I don't feel like I've had a proper natter with her in *ages*."

All of a sudden, Sonja felt a little ripple of uneasiness shoot up her spine. Considerate as Cat was being at this moment, maybe discussing Kerry with her wasn't such a great idea. It was probably safer to change the subject again.

"Speaking of all that university stuff," said Cat, "where have you applied to go? You've never told me."

"Mainly 'cause you're not usually interested in anything that doesn't directly involve *you*," said Sonja, resorting to the teasing tone the two girls usually used with each other. Anything rather than tell Cat the truth...

"Nah – go on, where do you want to go?"

"Why, will you miss me?" grinned Sonja, while she panicked for a suitable answer.

"Son! What's the big deal? Just tell me!"

Sonja pretended to be absorbed in looking for a scrunchie for her hair under the pile of newspapers on the kitchen table. It bought her a second or two.

"Look," she shrugged, pulling her blonde hair through the black scrunchie, "I looked at so many places, I can hardly remember where I've applied to. Anyway, that's not as important as Kerry. Do you *really* think she's unhappy?"

Sorry, Kerry, Sonja said silently to herself.

She'd betrayed her best friend, offering her up as a sacrifice to gossip. But at least it stopped Cat from going on at her.

Nobody but Sonja knew that the only application she was interested in was the one she'd sent to the university closest to Owen, and for the moment, that's how she wanted it to stay. If the others found out, then Anna would find out, and then Owen would find out too.

And if there was a chance that he was going to end up with Sonja living on his doorstep, then *she* was the only one he should hear it from.

If I ever get the courage to tell him...

CHAPTER 12

● ●

KERRY GETS A GRILLING

"How do you feel?"

"Awful. I've gone through a box of tissues in one day. I've never *seen* so much snot. It's disgusting."

"Well, Maya – you know this is all your own fault..."

"How do you make that one out?" Maya sniffed down the phone line.

"*You* were the one dragging us all out on to a freezing cold staircase two nights ago."

"Hmm. Well, it may just as well have been your mad boyfriend, dragging us all to the park when it was snowing."

Kerry looked in the hall mirror as they chatted, holding out one frizzy curl and wondering what she'd done in a past life to deserve such unruly hair. She was also wondering what she could do to keep this conversation going a while longer; she could hear how tired Maya sounded. But the sooner she came off the phone, the sooner she'd have to go through and talk to her parents.

When she'd come down from her room to grab a drink from the fridge five minutes earlier, her mum had called out from the living room and asked her to pop in; that's when Kerry had had to think fast and came up with the excuse that she had to phone Maya first.

Pity I can't keep Maya on the phone for the next few hours till they go to bed... she pondered, wrinkling her nose up at her reflection.

"I'm just glad this has happened while we're on holiday, so I don't have to worry about being off sixth form," Maya continued, her nose sounding all bunged up.

"You're mad!" Kerry burst out. "Most other people would be moaning about missing a great skiving opportunity!"

"Oh, don't make me sound like a swot! Now you've made me feel bad about being boring, as well as totally ill!"

"I'm sorry – I'm only joking," Kerry apologised, more contrite about the way she was using her friend than the idle teasing going on.

"I should let you get back to the sofa and your mound of snotty hankies..."

"Mmm, I better go – I'm starting to feel dizzy from standing so long. But thanks for phoning, Kerry and I'll see you later in the week once I'm germ-free."

"Sure. Take care of yourself. Bye..."

Kerry stared at the receiver once she'd put it back in place, then looked up into the mirror; without her contacts in or her glasses on, her reflection had a soft-focus edge to it.

She was glad of the blurriness; it meant she couldn't make out so clearly that look of dread she knew was written on her face. And if she was about to get a hard time from her parents, she'd rather see their faces through a comforting fuzz than in sharp detail.

• • •

"...And then I said to your dad, there's Jenny at work going on about what her daughter's plans are, and I feel guilty because we haven't really spoken about it much with you, and I don't want you to think we're not interested, Kerry."

Kerry sat perched on the arm of the chair nearest the living room door, as if she was ready for a quick getaway. Her mum and dad, sitting on the other armchair and the sofa respectively, were both gazing at her a little too intently for her liking. And worse still, they'd turned the telly down, so she knew they meant business.

"I know you're interested, Mum; you don't have to be on my back all the time to prove it," said Kerry, wishing with all her might that Lewis would wake up and come trotting down the stairs for a drink of water. Or that an urgent warning about tidal waves would flash up on the TV screen and tell everyone in Winstead to evacuate their houses now. *Anything* to get her parents off this particular subject.

"So what's happening with your applications? Did you get enough help from that careers advisor of yours?" asked her dad, pushing up his specs as he spoke. Kerry had not only inherited her poor eyesight from him, but also his habit of fiddling with his glasses when he was preoccupied. Obviously, he and Kerry's mum had been feeling this chat with their daughter was long overdue.

"Everything's sorted; don't worry," Kerry tried to pacify them.

"But when do you have to send these applications in by? Have you sent them already? What happens next?" her mum persisted.

"Mum – I'm still on holiday. I don't really want to think about all this stuff right now. Can we talk about it another time?" Kerry smiled at her pleadingly.

"But why? We just want to know what's happening with you," said her father. "What's the problem with just keeping us up to date?"

Kerry's mind was in a whirl – should she tell them her secret? How would they respond? She was on the verge of blurting it out, getting it off her chest, when she panicked.

"I just don't need this hassle right now," Kerry surprised herself by snapping and got up to leave.

"Kerry! What's all this about? Has this got something to do with Ollie?"

Her mother's words stopped her in her tracks and Kerry realised she was trembling. She never normally had run-ins with her parents – just the odd few niggles maybe – and it shocked her to see how shocked *they* were by her overwrought response to their questions.

"What do you mean about Ollie?" she asked, wondering how they could know what was going on inside her mind.

"Well, you spend an awful lot of time together. I mean, we have spoken about this before, Kerry, but you're not getting too serious, are you?"

Kerry felt her face flush with embarrassment.

"Do you mean, am I *sleeping* with him?" she gasped.

At the back of her mind, she knew she should be relieved that they hadn't really got an idea of what was on her mind after all, but the reality of what they were thinking was even more cringingly awful.

"No, no, it's not that," said her father placatingly. "It's just that maybe you and Ollie—"

"Graeme, wait a minute," interrupted Kerry's mum, holding her hand up and taking charge of the situation. "Yes, Kerry, it is about sleeping with him and maybe being too influenced by him, and forgetting about the rest of your life because you're so wrapped up in him, and even putting yourself in danger..."

"In danger? How?"

"Well, going out on that old motorbike of his," her dad interjected. "I saw him out on it last week, outside his parents' pub, and it was making a terrible racket. We aren't happy about you travelling on that thing. It isn't safe."

Kerry blinked hard. The tears of indignation threatening to well up in her eyes were making her vision even more blurred.

"For your information, we *aren't* sleeping together; Ollie *isn't* taking over my life..." Kerry crossed her fingers behind her back as she spoke the last part out loud "...and I *will* go out on his bike if I want to!"

"Kerry!" her mother called as she ran out of the room.

"Leave her..." she heard her father say.

If only... Kerry wished, running up the stairs to her room and slamming the door. *If only they'd leave me alone to lead my own life!*

With her heart pounding and her back pressed firmly against the door, Kerry's eyes strayed to her wardrobe, where the plastic bag was now hidden...

CHAPTER 13

• •

MISTAKEN IDENTITY

Ollie looked down at his watch as discreetly as he could. His parents would be expecting him downstairs in the bar at any minute, to help them get the glasses and the mixers stocked up for opening time at 11.00 am. But he could hardly interrupt Matt as he poured out his tale of woe.

"I didn't have a clue. Not one clue *that* was coming."

"Course you didn't! But there's no point in thinking that if you'd seen the signs earlier, you could've done something about it!" Ollie tried to reassure his friend.

He'd found out what had happened to Matt the previous evening, when Joe had rung to tell him. He was pleased that Matt felt he could come round and talk the whole break-up thing over with him – Ollie just wished it wasn't at half past ten on a Monday morning when he was needed elsewhere.

"What did Gabrielle *want*? For me to act like I didn't care? Well, I could easily have played it that way, if I'd known," Matt snapped bitterly, drumming his leg in agitation.

The drumming was causing small seismic rumblings across the bedroom floor. As discreetly as he could, Ollie reached over and grabbed his saxophone from where it was resting precariously against the chest of drawers, in danger of tipping over from the excess vibration rumbling over the carpet.

"You don't mean that," said Ollie, placing the sax gently on the bed behind him. "You were great together – you know you were. It just didn't work out, that's all."

"Saying I was too serious! Can you believe that?" yelped Matt.

Ollie suddenly realised that he was wasting his time trying to come up with words of wisdom: Matt wasn't in the right frame of mind to listen. All he wanted was someone to sit quietly and nod occasionally.

Wonder how Kerry's getting on? Ollie's thoughts drifted off. *It was great of Joe to ask her to go with him to his dad's, instead of her sitting at home 'cause I'm working and everyone else is doing stuff.*

Flickers of concern had been passing through Ollie's mind recently. Kerry seemed a little withdrawn and the last time that had happened was when she'd got herself all wound up about their relationship.

That had nearly ended with them breaking up – all because Kerry was too shy to tell him how she was feeling, and Ollie didn't want to go through that agony again.

Part of him hoped this was nothing, but another part of him hoped that if there was anything bothering her, she might open up to Joe about it. Ollie trusted Joe to set her straight, that was for sure.

Yep, I can rely on Joe... he told himself as Matt carried on with his outpourings of misery.

"What do you think?" said Matt suddenly, breaking into his friend's thoughts.

Ollie froze – he hadn't heard a word for the last minute or two.

"Well," he said, getting ready to waffle, "I think you should—"

"All she had to do was *say* something earlier! Why didn't she say? I'd have done anything she wanted!"

Ollie patted Matt on the back and kept his mouth shut.

● ● ●

"Wow – I forgot how pretty this place was!" said Kerry, stepping down from the bus into the picturesque village square. "Last time I was here was with my parents when Lewis was still really tiny."

"Yeah?" said Joe dubiously, glancing around him. He'd always thought that the village his dad had set up home in was too cutesy; too chocolate-box for his taste. But now, with a light sprinkling of pristine white snow clinging to the rooftops and tree branches, Joe could almost see its charm.

"Where to now?" Kerry smiled at him, her eyes wide with the excitement of being somewhere different.

"Just down this turning," he pointed, leading the way.

Joe still felt small jitters of nervousness, even though the nearly hour-long bus journey had been fine. They'd talked mostly about Matt and what might have led to his 'sacking' by Gabrielle.

"Which one's your dad's house?" asked Kerry eagerly, gazing in turn at the six or seven buildings dotted along the dead-end turning.

"The last one, with the white fence," Joe indicated with a nod. "The one with my dad at the window waving, actually."

By the time Joe and Kerry reached the gate, Joe's dad was rushing up the path towards them – a welcoming beam on his face – while Gillian stood smiling behind him in the doorway.

Joe gave Kerry a quick sideways glance as they walked through the gate and saw the slight look of surprise on her face.

What's she thinking? he wondered.

• • •

"So, do you think Joe looks like his father?" asked Gillian.

Kerry watched the two of them up ahead on the woodland path, heads nodding earnestly as they listened to each other talking, their shoulders similarly hunched. She'd never met Joe's dad before: his parents had split up long before Kerry knew him properly, and Joe hadn't seen much of his father since. Not until recently, when the ice between the two Gladwin men had finally begun to thaw.

"Yes, he does a bit," Kerry replied.

What had surprised her more was the resemblance between Gillian and Joe's mum – Susie – whom she knew reasonably well; they both had the same round, doll-like face and cosy, friendly manner.

No wonder it was so difficult for Joe to handle this, she thought as they strolled. *It would be hard enough if your dad left for someone the complete opposite of your mother, but when she's a carbon copy, only several years younger...*

Kerry liked Joe's mum – there wasn't a lot not to like. She welcomed all Joe's friends with the same bubbly enthusiasm and never stopped trying to force coffees, Cokes and three-course meals on everyone who stepped over the threshold. For Joe she could be a bit stifling – the others wouldn't have been surprised if she'd brought out a hankie and started wiping his face.

But then any mother who lets her son practise drums in his room can't be all bad, Kerry thought to herself, then immediately remembered the awkward silence between herself and her *own* mother at home that morning before she left.

Her mum had been pottering around Lewis, directing all her conversation at him and not his sister. Kerry was quite glad of it at the time – she couldn't bear a confrontation so early in the day – but couldn't quite stop wondering now whether that silence was due to her mum giving her a bit of space after the previous night's fall-out, or if it was simply because she was too angry to talk to her daughter.

"Have you and Joe known each other long?" Gillian smiled at her.

"Yeah, quite a while. Me and my friends got to know him through Ollie. Have you met Ollie?"

"That's the friend Joe's known since he was little, isn't it?"

Kerry nodded.

"No, I haven't met Ollie, but Joe's dad's mentioned him; he's told me lots about Joe's childhood. I mean, I've really only got to know *Joe* properly over the last few months. It was hard enough to get just him and his father together the first couple of years or so after his parents split up. Understandably enough."

"I guess so..." said Kerry, thinking how difficult it must have been for Gillian to be happy while living under the shadow of being the woman-who-stole-Joe's-dad-away for such a long time. But it still felt a little strange to Kerry to be on the brink of such a delicate subject with a woman she'd only just met.

"It's lovely to see them together like that," Gillian nodded up the snow-speckled path towards father and son. "And it's lovely that he felt comfortable enough to bring you."

A wave of confusion hit Kerry. The conversation had taken a very intimate turn and she wasn't sure why.

"I think Joe's dad in particular is really pleased that Joe wanted to bring his girlfriend to meet us,"

Gillian beamed, reaching out and patting Kerry lightly on the back.

"Oh!" squeaked Kerry in alarm.

Up ahead, Joe and his dad glanced back to see the cause of it. Kerry gave them a fleeting wave and hoped her face wasn't too red – the last thing she wanted right now was for them to hang back and wait for her.

Luckily, Joe just grinned back and they carried on walking.

"Oh, no, it's not like that!" she blustered. "Me and Joe are just friends! I go out with Ollie. Joe just asked me along today because..."

Kerry blushed furiously and didn't know what else to say. *Now* she knew why Gillian had been talking so openly to her.

"Kerry, I'm so sorry! What an idiot I am – putting two and two together and coming up with six and a half!" giggled Gillian, immediately putting Kerry at her ease.

"That's OK. I'd have probably thought the same thing," Kerry reassured her, feeling the flush begin to subside.

Me and Joe together – what a funny idea! thought Kerry, her tummy giving a little ripple of embarrassment at the very idea. *If Joe knew that's what his dad and Gillian had assumed, he'd be absolutely mortified!*

• • •

Kerry wiped a circle of condensation away from the steamed-up window of the bus and waved at the couple huddled companionably together on the pavement.

Joe squashed up beside her as he mouthed a self-conscious 'bye' at his father and Gillian, who was waving.

"Sorry, Kez..." he said as the bus rumbled into life and he bashed shoulders with her.

"Don't be silly!" she smiled.

Suddenly Kerry had an overwhelming desire to wrap her arms around her friend and give him an enormous cuddle; she could have spent the day mooching uselessly in her room, but instead, thanks to Joe, she'd had a totally unexpected, brilliant day out.

"Thanks for asking me along," she said, in lieu of the cuddle. "I had such a nice time. Your dad's great. They're *both* great."

Joe beamed for a second then switched his expression to 'worried'.

"But you don't have to come next Sunday, Kerry, if you don't want to," he said hurriedly, referring to his dad's last-minute invitation as they both boarded the bus. "I mean, I know I'll be coming out for a driving lesson, but that might not be too interesting for you. And Ollie, of course."

Kerry had been relieved when Joe tagged Ollie's name on to the invitation – even without being aware of the assumption his father had made about his son and herself.

"Course I'd love to come again! And I'm sure Ollie would love to see your dad after all this time," Kerry reassured him. Ollie, she knew, would happily do anything it took to make his friend's life easier, and greasing the wheels of Joe's relationship with his dad sounded like the perfect way to help.

Joe shuffled in his seat, looking pleased and slightly awkward at the same time.

"And you know something, Joe?" Kerry began, feeling very close to him all of a sudden.

Blinking at her anxiously, Joe wondered what was coming next.

"Seeing the three of you getting on so well today, after – I s'pose – *everything* was really nice. It just..." Kerry shook her head a little, making her curls bob dizzily around her face, "...kind of put things in perspective for me."

"How?" asked Joe, scanning her face for clues.

"Oh, I just had a sort of run-in with my mum and dad last night – over something and nothing – and it just seems a bit stupid now."

Now that she'd said it, Kerry almost wished she hadn't. She certainly didn't want to get any further into this subject – and the secret that lay behind it – even with sweet, dependable Joe.

CHAPTER 14

● ●

STORMY WEATHER

"Matt, I know you're not a happy bunny right now, but can you just think of something else for a second? And *please* stop doing that, babe!"

Sonja wrestled the teaspoon from Matt's hand and planted a sympathetic kiss on his cheek. He'd been staring into space, absently clanging the spoon on the side of his empty coffee mug and setting everyone's teeth on edge for the last five minutes.

"Yeah, you got dumped – get over it," yawned Cat.

None of the others looked taken aback at her tactlessness or told her off like they normally would have. Having been dumped herself – and pretty rudely – by Matt in the dim, distant past, she almost had a right now to have a dig.

"Come on, Matt – you're a party animal. Normally. What can we do to make Anna's birthday special?"

Matt looked at Sonja with dewy eyes, the very mention of making someone's birthday special hitting him right where it hurt.

"OK, OK, we'll let you off," said Sonja, patting her silent friend on the arm. "Go back to staring out the window – but just leave off with the tapping."

Instead, Matt stared round the café table at his friends – Sonja and Cat, Kerry and Joe, who'd come straight from the bus station to the End this Monday teatime – and stood up suddenly, sending cups and glasses clattering across the Formica.

"Sorry, got to go..." he announced, stony-faced.

"What was that all about?" asked Kerry as the door slammed shut.

"Karma," said Cat.

"What are you on about?" Sonja frowned at her.

"Karma – what goes around comes around. Matt's just suffering from the indignity of being chucked for the first time in his life, after spending years chucking every girl who's had the misfortune to fall for *him*," Cat suggested, hardly able to hide her triumphant smile.

"Um, Natasha blew him out too, remember..." Joe muttered.

"Of course she did!" smirked Cat, immediately remembering Ollie's twin sister. "How fabulous! Poor old Matt; it's a bad day on the planet for him, but I can't help enjoying it."

"Well, I guess you're entitled to gloat a *little* bit," shrugged Sonja, "but what he did to you was a long time ago and he *is* supposed to be a friend, so don't overdo it."

"Spoilsport..." Cat grumbled under her breath.

"Listen, this isn't getting us anywhere. What are we going to do about Anna's birthday?" Sonja hissed, glancing over at the entrance to the kitchen and getting ready to signal everyone to change the subject if she saw Anna come back out.

"Maybe..." Joe began, feeling on a high after the success of his day out with Kerry.

"Yes?" said Sonja.

"Maybe we could sneak into her flat while she was working. Do it up – balloons, streamers and stuff."

"Brilliant idea!" squealed Sonja.

In a flash, she saw them all transforming Anna's pretty living room into a fairylight-strewn grotto, with everyone hiding, ready to pounce on her as soon as she came though the door, tired from a long, hard shift and expecting nothing more than a dull night in front of Monday night telly. The thought *also* occurred to her that it might be interesting to glance around Anna's flat in her absence – maybe it would throw up a few clues to whatever Owen had been hinting at the day before. About Anna's less-then-easy life.

"We could get the key off Nick," Sonja started to plan, her eyes glinting with excitement. "He is her landlord after all. And then we could—"

"Are you *crazy?*"

Sonja stopped with her hands in mid-air and stared at Kerry, even though she couldn't believe that angry little growl had come from her best friend.

"What?" shrugged Sonja.

"That's trespass, Son! I can't believe you think that's a good idea!"

Joe, sitting next to Kerry, sank deep down into his seat.

"It's not trespass – it's a surprise, Kerry; just a nice surprise. Like when you were all in on the fact that Owen was coming up this weekend and didn't let on," Sonja tried to pacify her.

"It's *not* the same," Kerry snapped, her face white and tense. "It's invading someone's privacy and it's not fair!"

Sonja could see that Kerry's hands were trembling – raising her voice wasn't something that came naturally to her. She didn't know quite what to say.

"Sorry, I– I've got to go," mumbled Kerry, grabbing up her bag and shuffling out of the booth without a backward glance at her friends.

"How exciting!" said Cat, clapping her hands together. "Which one of us is going to storm out next?"

"Give it a rest," Sonja snarled, wondering whether she should go after Kerry or leave it till later to call her and find out what was wrong.

Joe sat silently on the other side of the table from the cousins and wondered how such a brilliant day could turn out so badly.

I should have stuck to the list, he berated himself. *I ditched it after a day and look how miserable I feel...*

● ● ●

What did I over-react like that for? What must they all think of me? Kerry fretted.

Her key was being stubborn and refusing to turn in the lock.

"Come *on!*" she said under her breath, yanking the troublesome bit of metal back and forth. Finally, there was a clunk and she found herself practically tripping into the front hall of her house.

Poor Joe, she winced as she thundered up the stairs. *He must think I'm such a bitch. That idea to sneak into Anna's flat was his – and I just flipped. And after him being so sweet and taking me to his dad's and everything!*

There in front of her was her bedroom door: sanctuary. In seconds, she'd be in her room, where she could calm down and try and sort out the mess in her head.

"Mum!"

Trisha Bellamy was crouching down by the open bottom drawer of her daughter's dressing table.

"Why are you constantly snooping all the time! What are you trying to find?"

"Kerry, I..." her mum looked quizzically at her.

"Why can't you just leave me alone?"

Her mother rushed over to her – still clutching the ironing she'd been putting away – as Kerry burst into tears.

CHAPTER 15

● ●

MATT TRIES AGAIN

"I forgive you... No, no."

Matt shook his head. It sounded too pompous.

"Now that you've had time to think, do you see...?" Matt's sentence trailed away.

See what? See that she made a big mistake? he questioned himself. *Wow, now I sound like a headmaster. Yeah, she's really going to see that I'm a fun guy if I come out with that!*

Having just manoeuvred his car into a space outside Gabrielle's terraced house, Matt turned off the ignition. Immediately, the car bucked forward, narrowly missing the bumper of the van parked in front.

Swearing under his breath and with trickles of sweat beginning to form on his forehead, Matt pushed the clutch down and yanked the gearstick into neutral, as he should have done in the first place. It showed how distracted he was; Matt prided himself on being a good driver, not some novice who left the car in gear before switching off the engine.

Maybe I should just give her a look... he thought, getting out of the door and locking it behind him. *Maybe a long, lingering look will say more than words ever can...*

Preparing his face for The Look, Matt took a deep breath and rang the doorbell.

"Oh, hi, Matt. I guess you want to see Gaby?"

Matt couldn't find his voice, but managed to nod at Simone, Gabrielle's older sister. He'd seen her briefly just a couple of weeks before, when she'd picked up Gaby in town, after she and Matt had been Christmas shopping. That day, Simone had just finished her shift as receptionist at the River Road fitness centre, where Matt and Gabrielle had first met, when Matt was DJing on its opening night.

Jiggling his car keys in his hand, Matt peered round the partially open door into the hall of the house while he waited. He'd never been inside; only ever got as far as the spot where his car was now parked, on the many occasions he'd dropped Gaby home. She'd said she wasn't into the idea of taking him in and introducing him to her parents; told him it was all too 'serious', he remembered now.

She'd been to *his* house plenty of times – hanging out in his den, lazing in the garden (until the weather turned colder), sprawling on the sofa watching videos on the huge TV in his living room. "It's not the same, though, is it?" she'd said to him by way of explanation. "Your dad's never there, and when he is, you two live more like flatmates than father and son anyway."

He hadn't got his head round her reasoning then, and he certainly didn't now. It was crazy that of all the girls he'd been out with, the only one whose parents he'd have been happy to meet were Gabrielle's and she wasn't up for it. The only glimpse he'd had of them was the back of her dad's head, on the couple of occasions he'd come to pick up Gabrielle from parties where Matt was DJing and couldn't see her home.

"Matt?"

Gabrielle slipped out of the front door and pulled it nearly closed behind her.

For a second, his mind went blank. In the three days he hadn't seen her, he'd forgotten quite how pretty she was. She stood, small and delicate, her arms folded against the cold – and Matt – across her chest. Her braids and beads were scooped up into a ponytail, with just one lone braid dangling by her face. Her eyes, big and brown, looked up searchingly into his.

"Why, Gaby?" was the only thing that came out of his mouth. Loudly. Angrily.

Gabrielle glanced up and down the street, as if curious neighbours might be lurking in every window.

"Matt – what are you doing here?" she asked him nervously.

"What am I doing here?" he repeated incredulously. "What am I *doing* here? What do you think I'm doing? I'm trying to understand why you finished with me, just like that!"

Matt snapped his fingers in front of her face, making her jump.

"Please, Matt, I explained the other night—"

"What kind of explanation was that? That I'm no fun? How can you say you love me one minute and then finish with me for such a stupid reason?"

"Well, it's how I feel! I can't help it! I still love you but—"

"You still love me?" gasped Matt, his stomach flipping at her words. Was there still a chance?

"Not– not like I did... I just don't think we're right together."

"Why? *Why* aren't we right?" Matt demanded, his hurt nearly breaking his heart.

"Matt, please – please just go..." begged Gabrielle, pulling her arms tighter around her chest.

"But Gab—"

The door behind her flew open and a towering man stood behind Gabrielle's slender frame.

"What's all this shouting about?"

"Dad, it's OK, it's just Matt..."

"Oh, *you're* the one she's been seeing," he glowered.

Matt ignored him, staring intently at Gabrielle's beautiful face.

"Get in the house," the older man ordered.

"Gaby!" Matt shouted as she retreated into the shadowy hall.

"You – get lost," Gabrielle's father bellowed. "No one comes round here upsetting my daughter!"

The slam of the door echoed round Matt's head as he turned and dragged himself away.

CHAPTER 16

●●●●●●●●●●●●●●●●●●●●●●●●●●●●

ON THE SPOT

"Orange juice, just like you requested, Madame!"

"Thanks, Billy," Maya smiled at her friend.

Billy put his own drink on the table, plus one in front of Andy – The Loud's bass player – and pulled up a stool.

"Are you sure you're OK, Maya? You're still pretty sniffly..."

"Yes, I'm not too bad. I was just going mad staying at home. I haven't been out in nearly a week," said Maya, dabbing at her nose with a crumpled tissue. "Mind you, I don't know how long I'll last. It's really crowded and smoky in here tonight."

Billy and Andy gazed around at the packed pub and nodded.

"Looks like everyone got stir crazy after New

Year," nodded Billy. "Hope they're in the mood to listen to us play tonight."

"Well, they wouldn't have come otherwise, would they?" Maya pointed out. "You're the star attraction on Thursday nights at the Railway Tavern."

"Or maybe it's something to do with the fact that there's nothing else to do on a Thursday night in Winstead..." said Andy.

Maya smiled and took a sip of her orange juice. "Well, considering *I'm* the sickly one, I was the first to arrive – even before you two! I don't know where the others are."

Billy glanced down at his watch. Maya was right; everyone was cutting it fine. Although it was unusual, it didn't matter so much that Sonja, Cat, Anna and Kerry weren't there to keep Maya company and cheer on the band; it was more worrying that there was still no sign of Matt, who did their sound, and, of course, Joe and Ollie.

Nick was up at the bar now, Billy noticed, checking his watch too. He liked to think he was a laid-back bloke, but it was obvious he was getting twitchy.

A flurry of activity at the door heralded one bunch of missing friends. Maya gave them a wave to alert them to where she was sitting, with extra stools saved for them.

"Where have you been?" she asked as the girls got themselves settled, Billy and Andy standing up to make room for them.

"Don't ask," Sonja growled.

"OK, OK, so it was my fault!" said Cat, holding up her hands. "We were all meant to be meeting at Anna's flat, but it took me ages to get there."

"And *those* are the reason why..." Sonja explained, directing Maya's gaze towards Cat's feet.

Maya stared down at the elegant, strappy sandals, which would have looked gorgeous with tanned legs in summer, but were ridiculous in January worn with bare feet.

"Cat – you're mad! You'll get flu like I did!" exclaimed Maya, staring down. "Your toes are practically *purple* with the cold!"

"Yeah, I know," whimpered Cat. "But these are new and they're... pretty!"

"And what're *those*?" asked Maya, pointing to flashes of bright blue on Cat's mauve skin – one on her ankle and one where her sandal rubbed the top of her foot.

Cat lifted up one leg to show off the special coloured plasters, used particularly by the catering industry.

"They were all I had," said Anna. "I had to use my spare keys to open up the café and get them

128

out of the first-aid box. We had to stick *something* on those blisters Cat came limping in with."

"Anyway, are you feeling better, Maya?" Kerry leant over to ask. "We'd have told you to meet us at Anna's too if we'd known you were coming out tonight."

"Don't worry," Maya shrugged. "It was probably just as well I came here on my own or I wouldn't have been able to keep this table. But listen – do you know what's happened to Ollie and Joe and Matt? Andy and Billy are getting worried, not to mention Nick. He's practically eating his beer mat he's so tense."

Kerry shook her head. "They're not here? That's odd. Ollie didn't say anything was wrong when I spoke to him on the phone earlier. Didn't say they'd be late, either..."

"Well, that's a relief, I suppose," said Billy. "I was worried Ollie might have got flu like everyone else. When I called him earlier in the week he said half the staff at The Swan were down with it."

"God, everyone's ill at the moment, aren't they? Even Kerry's been feeling lousy," Sonja commented.

"Have you, Kerry? You never said..." Maya asked with concern.

Her question seemed to make Kerry squirm, she noticed.

"Just headaches and stuff."

"Yeah, she's been all ratty lately, haven't you?" Sonja joined in, giving her best friend a comforting rub on the arm. "Silly thing's been feeling bad for a while now and hadn't told me or Ollie or her folks what was up."

"Have you been to see my dad?" Maya asked.

It was strange for her knowing that her father was also Sonja and Kerry's GP. He knew confidential things about the girls that he would never contemplate divulging to his daughter, and she knew secrets about them that she'd never consider telling her dad – *ever.*

"Um, no... I think it's just some viral bug I've got or something," waffled Kerry.

Maya fixed her with a stare. The one thing she shared with her parents was a liking for being straightforward and practical. Which Kerry *wasn't* being at this precise moment.

"Kerry, you can't make a diagnosis on your own! If you've been feeling bad then you've got to—"

"Back in a minute!" said Kerry a little too brightly, as she got up and headed to the loos.

● ● ●

Just my luck to have Maya give me the third degree, Kerry thought, repositioning the butterfly clips that kept her curls pinned back from her face. The expression that looked back at her from the mirror in the not-very-sanitary Railway Tavern ladies' loos read 'rumbled', loud and clear. God – sometimes life was so complicated!

The lie that she'd thought up while her mother comforted her in her bedroom on Monday night – the one about suffering in silence with migraines – had washed OK with Sonja and Ollie, as well as with her apologetic parents. So well, in fact, that her mum and dad had been treating her with kid gloves. Only Maya – who was still genuinely poorly herself – could spot the flaws in her story. Typical!

Kerry sighed, walked over to the door and pulled it open, mentally preparing to go back to her table and face The Inquisition Part Two from Maya. Instead, she stumbled into the arms of a passing boy. Confounding her impression that all her luck was bound to be bad, she glanced up at the face belonging to the arms that had been thrown around her and realised she was staring up at her own boyfriend.

Ollie was so ridiculously cute – especially at such close quarters – that Kerry couldn't stop herself from blushing.

"Whoah! Where're you going in such a hurry!" he laughed, kissing her on the forehead, his floppy brown hair inadvertently tickling her face.

"I'm supposed to be watching this great band I've heard about! But someone told me they haven't shown up yet..." Kerry teased him. "No doubt they're trashing a dressing-room somewhere!"

"I know, I know – we're due on stage, like, *now*. But, uh, you wouldn't believe the hassle, Kez," Ollie sighed, all the good-humoured pretence ditched for a second. "Convincing Matt to come along tonight was a total nightmare. He's absolutely hit rock bottom over this split with Gabrielle. He was going to stay home doing this hermit thing till me and Joe bullied him into coming along."

Kerry, leaning her weight on to Ollie and balancing on tiptoe, looked over his shoulder and squinted over at the sound-mixing desk where Matt stood, hollow-cheeked and earnest, behind the numerous rows of buttons and knobs. It wasn't a happy picture.

"He doesn't look *too* bad," Kerry lied, hoping Matt – in the state he was obviously in – could make it through the night without landing his friends in a mess of whining feedback.

"Yeah, but how are *you*?" Ollie asked, his

eyebrows creasing as he stared intently into Kerry's face. "Have you made an appointment with Dr Joshi yet?"

Kerry shrugged apologetically.

"Tomorrow, promise. Um, Ollie..." she said, nervously stroking his face.

"What?" he asked, his eyes boring into hers,

"My parents have been getting at me lately..." she began.

"About what?"

The loud hubbub and music went on all around them in the pub, while Ollie and Kerry stood in their own little vortex.

"They've been hassling me about... about... being on the Vespa with you," Kerry found herself saying, even though it wasn't what she'd intended to talk about. "They think it's too dangerous."

"Are they crazy?" asked Ollie, the outrage written across his face. "Like I'd risk anything that could hurt *you*?"

"I know, I know," Kerry tried to reassure her boyfriend.

"I like your folks; I thought they liked – thought they trusted – me!" he yelped indignantly.

"Yeah, well," Kerry bit her lip guiltily. "There is something else—"

"Oh, my God!"

Kerry's heart did flip-flops till she realised Ollie's gaze was fixed at a point somewhere over her shoulder. She turned and peered in the direction of his startled gaze.

"Gaby..." she gasped, as Matt's ex strolled in though the entrance.

• • •

Joe gave thanks once again that the instrument that he shone on was the drums. Yeah, so he could strum away on the acoustic guitar he had in his bedroom – wrote all his tunes on it, in fact – but the drums were his true love.

And the best thing about being a drummer – the thing that suited Joe down to the ground – was that he was the one person least likely to be stared at in the band, hidden away behind his drum kit.

Except maybe tonight... Joe felt flustered, seeing a dark-haired girl – with the glint of a pretty nose ring – at the front of the stage shoot him a meaningful stare.

The day out with Kerry was what he'd needed, he'd already realised, to get her out of his system once and for all. His list hadn't been wasted; he'd had to have that one-on-one time to see that she was lovely, but not some unattainable princess. From here on in – especially after the strop she'd had on Monday night, when she'd stormed out of the End – it would be easy to put the list back into action.

7. Keep remembering the real love of my life could be passing me by, all because I'm so wrapped up in this obsession with Kerry...

Joe turned all this over in his mind as he clicked his drumsticks, counting in the first number. The dark-haired girl at the edge of the stage began to sway as Andy took up the infectious bass line. Her eyes still seemed fixed on Joe's...

Maybe she's the one I'm supposed to be with, he thought, shivers running down his back as he beat out the rhythm on the snare and the tom-toms.

Already, beads of sweat were forming on his hairline – partly through nerves at performing, partly due to the hot spotlights trained on the band from the lighting rig on the ceiling – but also partly through excitement at the girl watching him...

Maybe I should try and talk to her after the set, thought Joe, not losing an ounce of concentration for the tune he was playing. *Maybe...*

At that second Ollie – who was standing directly in front of Joe – bent double over the mike and then leant sideways, growling into the first line of the song.

She's watching Ollie! Joe suddenly realised, tracking the dark-haired girl's line of vision. *Of course it's not me!*

Strangely, he wasn't too disappointed. In his mind, it would have been surprising if out of the four of them – Ollie, with his obvious indie-boy good looks; Andy, with his black hair and killer cheekbones; Billy, all athletic muscles and white-toothed smile – Joe had attracted the admiring glances of such a pretty face as the dark-haired girl out front.

But at least it means I'm starting to get interested in other girls, he reassured himself. *There is life after Kerry...*

• • •

Matt tried to imagine he had blinkers on; that all he could see was what was straight ahead.

But no matter how hard he stared at The Loud over on the small stage in the corner of the pub, he couldn't help but see Gaby out of the corner of his eye, pushing her way through the packed room towards him.

"Matt!" she yelled above the music, pulling at his elbow to attract his attention.

Matt couldn't bear to look at her at that precise moment. Gazing into her pretty face would just open the wound all over again.

"What do you want?" he said, compromising by leaning down towards her to hear her words better, but flicking his eyes from the band to the mixing desk only.

"Matt, I have to talk to you!"

"I'm working," he said matter-of-factly, though his heart was cha-cha-cha-ing up and down his rib cage. "Couldn't you make it later?"

"No, I can't stay. My dad didn't want me to come out tonight – he thinks I've changed my mind and that I'm just going to be out trying to find you."

Matt didn't say anything. His hopes were beginning to rise and he could hardly breathe with the anticipation.

"But I had to come and see you – to say sorry, about my dad shouting at you and everything. It wasn't fair."

And everything? Matt wondered, still not daring to look at her in case... in case the desire to wrap his arms around her was too hard to resist.

"Matt, I know you're angry with me," her voice rang in his ear. She was leaning one hand on his shoulder as she spoke; he could feel the warmth of it practically burning its way through his shirt to his skin.

"I *was* angry," he found himself saying, finally fixing his eyes on hers. She had her hair scooped up again, same as she was wearing it when he'd gone round to her house on Monday.

It was all he could do to stop himself reaching out and touching the one braid that hung down, following the line of her neck, with its soft brown skin...

"Matt, I– I–" she said, blinking her long-lashed eyes up at him. "I didn't want you to hear this from anybody else... But I'm seeing someone."

His heart, well battered and bruised after a rotten week, took this new blow without any great surprise. Just total gut-wrenching disappointment.

"Who...?" he mumbled so quietly she couldn't hear, but managed to lip-read.

"No one you know," she shook her head sadly. "He's a neighbour. He goes to my school."

The instant, ear-splitting whine of feedback that suddenly emitted from Ollie's mike had all the punters in the Railway Tavern wincing and covering their ears.

The only one who didn't seem to notice the racket was Matt, whose hand was on the fader button that had caused it.

I've been blown out! Matt tried to take the information in. *Blown out for some kid!*

"What the hell are you doing, Matt?" Nick yelled. He'd lunged over from the bar to the sound desk in an attempt to save everyone's eardrums from irreparable damage.

But the indignity was too much. Matt turned and barged his way through the cringing crowds, unaware of Ollie yelling out his name from the stage.

CHAPTER 17

• •

ESPECIALLY FOR YOU...

Sonja gave Ollie a wave, mouthed "It'll be OK!" at him and headed towards the door, pulling her coat on as she went. Anna had already disappeared out into the chilly January night, in hot pursuit of Matt.

Ollie glanced over at Nick, who'd torn off his jacket and was trying to familiarise himself with the desk. There was no point in the band stopping – too many people would be let down, including the Railway Tavern's manager, who might just be tempted to ditch their regular spot if the boys messed up. Ollie glanced round at Billy, Andy and Joe, nodded his head as he counted in the next song and hoped the atmosphere wouldn't be too flattened by what had happened.

"No sign of Gaby!" Maya said to Kerry, taking her seat at the table again.

Maya had tried to make her way over to Gabrielle as soon as they saw Matt's hasty exit, but by the time she'd weaved through the crowd, Matt's ex was nowhere to be seen. After checking out the toilets, Maya had had to admit defeat and come back to her seat.

"I hope she's all right! I hope *he's* all right!" Kerry bit her lip. "God, hasn't it been a weird night?"

Maya nodded. For her, the whole evening was taking on a surreal edge, mostly, she knew, due to the after-effects of flu making her feel wobbly on this first night out. But Matt storming out was pretty unsettling, as was Kerry's mood. She seemed preoccupied and there was definitely something suspect about that migraine story. Kerry didn't look ill – just worried.

Those two factors aside, what was also freaking Maya out was the fact that when she'd come back from her fruitless search for Gaby, she'd found Cat flanked by Rudi and Marc. That wasn't strange in itself; it was more that they stopped their heads-together whispering as soon as Maya approached them.

Not being particularly prone to paranoia, Maya would have thought no more of it if Cat hadn't been wearing her Cheshire Cat grin – the one that let everyone know she was up to something.

"What do you think's going on with Cat and those lads?" Maya asked Kerry.

Kerry snuck a peek at their friend. "Don't know, but she's got that look, hasn't she?"

"That's what's worrying me..."

Just then, their attention was caught by the sight of Rudi walking past them, threading his way through the tables directly in front of the stage, and waving a scrap of paper at Ollie.

Ollie, still singing, looked confused, but took the piece of paper from him. He flipped it open, smiled broadly, and carried on with the song.

As Rudi wended his way back, Maya turned and gave Cat a questioning stare.

"What was all that about?" she mouthed.

Cat shrugged unconvincingly, then began talking animatedly with Marc.

"You're right – tonight *is* totally weird," Maya said to Kerry. "Wonder what's going to happen next?"

Applause exploded all around them as the appreciative audience cheered the end of the song.

"Thanks," Ollie's words echoed through the mike. "Right, the next one's a dedication – we've never done one of these before – and it's going out to a friend of ours, actually!"

Maya and Kerry swapped intrigued glances.

"So here we go. This is a little song of ours called – appropriately enough – *If Only You Knew*, and it's going out to Maya..."

Maya felt a rush so hot it was as if she'd been dipped in boiling water.

"...with lots of love from Rudi..."

CHAPTER 18

● ●

OLLIE BAILS OUT

"Hands off, Ravi," said Maya, pulling the packet of condoms her little brother was fiddling with out of his hands and putting it back on the rack.

"But, Maya, what are—"

"I'll just be a minute talking to Kerry," his sister interrupted his awkward question, "and then we'll go to Burger King, all right?"

Kerry and Maya rolled their eyes at each other and tried to carry on their conversation.

"Anyway, so Cat actually apologised?" asked Kerry, pricing bottles of shampoo as they spoke. Her boss at the chemist's where she worked on Saturdays – Mr Hardy – was pretty cool about friends dropping in occasionally. He only got grumpy if the shop was busy or if chats went on and on when there were shelves to fill.

"Yes – she phoned last night; I could hardly believe it. Just said sorry if the dedication thing embarrassed me."

"*Embarrassed* you? That's an understatement – I've never seen you go so beetroot!"

"Well, what could I do?" Maya was able to laugh, now that a couple of days had passed since the incident. "It would have been a lot easier if Cat had just told me Rudi liked me, instead of encouraging the poor lad to go through that whole humiliating scene."

"Oooh," Kerry winced at the memory. "The way all those people in the pub were staring at you!"

"And the way I had to let him down... saying thanks but no thanks. His little face!" Maya covered her own face as she remembered the excruciating few minutes after Ollie had read out what was written in Rudi's note. "I felt so bad!"

"No wonder you left just after that..."

"And he left just after me?" Maya double-checked, going over what Kerry had told her on the phone.

"Yeah. His mate and Cat went out after him."

"First Matt and Gabrielle and then me and Rudi – what an emotional night!"

"I know, but..." smirked Kerry.

"But what?" asked Maya, pulling Ravi's

inquisitive fingers away from where they were straying.

Kerry grinned wickedly. "Well, you must – even just in a little way – feel flattered by it!"

Maya looked indignant for a second and then found herself grinning too.

"OK, so I am a *bit* flattered," she admitted. "But I'd rather not have had to go through all that."

"But it's nice to be fancied, even if it's by someone you don't fancy back."

Maya shrugged. She had plenty of experience of boys as mates, but when it came to romance, she could be described as a non-starter. She hadn't ever been out on more than one date with anyone, hadn't ever found a boy she felt strongly about.

That wasn't to say she was naive about love and relationships; she'd seen enough of her friends messing up to know that being patient and selective wasn't doing her any harm.

"You know something?" said Kerry, picking up a bundle of bottles and coming out from behind the counter.

Maya, pulling Ravi by the hand, followed her friend down to the front of the shop, where she began to fill the empty spaces in the shampoo section.

"What's that then?" Maya asked.

"You know how three's a lucky number?"

Maya nodded, wondering what Kerry was getting at.

"Well, last year, Billy was after you. Now you find out Rudi's got a thing for you," Kerry explained. "And I know you weren't interested in either of them that way, but I think that the next person is going to be the right person for you..."

"Thank you, Mystic Meg," laughed Maya. "But I can't say I believe in your theory."

"Oh, look, here's Ollie," said Kerry as a sharp knock at the window attracted their attention. "Let's ask him what he thinks about my idea!"

"No thanks! I think it's time me and Ravi got a move on anyway..."

Ollie peeked in round the door, winked at Ravi, and ran up behind Kerry, tickling her till she squealed.

"Don't – you'll get me into trouble!" she shrieked, looking over in a panic to check Mr Hardy wasn't around.

"Come on, Ravi – these people are too childish for you and me," said Maya with a smile as she pulled open the door. "See you two later!"

"Bye, Maya, bye, Ravi," chorused Kerry and Ollie.

"Maya?" they heard a little voice say. "What was in those little packets on the counter?"

"Um, cough sweets..." they heard Maya say, before the door closed behind her.

Ollie and Kerry tried to hide their sniggers.

"It's not often you hear Maya tell porky-pies!" laughed Ollie.

"Well, we all have our moments..." Kerry muttered, her good spirits fading away. They faded even further when Ollie carried on.

"Listen, this day out to Joe's tomorrow..."

"Oh, Ollie! You're not blowing Joe out, are you?"

"Kez – I can't help it!" Ollie looked at her pleadingly. "My dad's got flu now. I've got to help Mum out at the pub!"

"Of course you do..." she admitted. "I'm just disappointed. I had a lovely day out there last week and I thought you'd really enjoy it. And Joe would have loved you to be there too."

"I know... But at least he'll have you," Ollie shrugged.

Kerry felt flustered. For some reason, no matter how nice a time she'd had before, it felt too strange to be heading off alone with Joe again. "I can't go on my own, Ol!"

"Don't be silly, Kerry! You went on your own last time. And anyway, you're just as much Joe's friend as I am!"

"Of course," Kerry smiled.

"Right, I've got to run – Nick'll skin me alive for being late at the End," said Ollie hurriedly, kissing her swiftly on the nose.

Kerry lifted a bottle of shampoo and distractedly waved him goodbye with it.

● ● ●

I'd love it if I could tell someone what I've done, without worrying that they'll tell me off, Kerry mused as she kicked off her shoes after a hard day's serving and collapsed on her bed.

She let one hand drop off the side, where it curled round Barney's wet snout. The dog snuffled with happiness, then panted off to explore the room he'd been shut out of all day.

Maybe I should talk to Joe about it tomorrow – he wouldn't be all judgmental or tell me I was being stupid...

The minute the thought crossed her mind, Kerry felt bad.

The first person I have to tell is Ollie, since it affects him, she realised. *It's just that I know he's going to be mad at me...*

A rustling sound interrupted her thoughts.

"Barney, what are you doing?" she sighed, pushing herself up on her elbows to peer in the direction of the noise.

Barney looked up with a guilty expression and a tongue lolling pathetically from the side of his mouth.

The plastic bag he'd been playing with – dragged from the bottom of the wardrobe – lay ripped in the middle of the carpet. Envelopes, with stamps visible on them, spilled out of the largest tear.

"Shoo!" Kerry yelped, throwing herself off the bed and on to the floor and sending Barney scurrying off.

From his position of safety, just outside the room, the dog stole a nervous look around the bedroom door – only to see his mistress sitting staring dolefully at a bunch of half-chewed letters in her lap...

CHAPTER 19

• •

ONE WRONG MOVE

The view from the top of the lane was stunning. The snow-topped hills to the east were just visible above the trees, and to the west, the frost-covered fields dipped up and down over the uneven countryside.

"Look – see the tip of the spire there? That's the village."

Kerry nodded; she could just make it out through the tall branches.

Somewhere out on the small roads around them, Joe was getting his first driving lesson with his father, while Kerry and Gillian had wrapped up and gone for a walk in the winter sunshine. Kerry thought it was achingly beautiful.

"You're so lucky to live here, Gillian!"

The young woman smiled ruefully. "Well,

I know that now, but when we first moved here, it felt like being sent into exile..."

She began walking again, striding down the quiet, winding road that would take them back to the bungalow.

"What do you mean?" asked Kerry, falling into step by her side.

"Well, Winstead can be a pretty small place. When I got together with Bobby – Joe's dad – we realised we were going to have to move away, if we didn't want to be the talk of the whole town."

"Really?"

"Oh, yes. Understandably, everyone was very sympathetic to Joe's mum and a lot of people know her through working at the health centre. Then there was the uncomfortable atmosphere at work, when people found out, plus, of course, my parents weren't very happy."

Kerry hadn't thought of the wider implications of the situation. When Joe had told them about his dad running off with his secretary – which had happened a few years before the girls had got to know Joe properly – Kerry had imagined that only four people were involved: Joe, his parents and Gillian as the other woman.

"So your parents flipped about you falling in love with a married man?"

"That and the fact that he was so much older than me," Gillian laughed, accentuating her round apple cheeks and bright eyes. "I was only twenty-three when it all happened."

Only six years older than I am now. Kerry did a quick calculation. *She had to put up with all that grief over the man she loved...*

Suddenly, Kerry didn't feel like the only person in the world doing something drastic for love. Suddenly, she felt as though she had found someone to talk everything over with; someone who'd understand and not criticise.

"It's funny that you're telling me all this 'cause my parents have got a bit of a downer on Ollie at the moment," she began, feeling dizzy now that she was on the verge of spilling the secret she'd been keeping for so long.

"Really? What have they been saying?"

"Oh, lots of stuff..." Kerry shrugged, not sure where to start. "They're making a big deal about stupid things like me going out on the back of his bike with him – they say it's not safe. And Mum's gone on a few times about, well – the sex thing. And I don't think she believes me when I've said we haven't... y'know, *done* it."

"Well, that's just normal parent angst, isn't it?" Gillian smiled.

"It's more than that," Kerry waffled, taking the

long way round to her confession. "I've done something they're going to go totally mad at..."

• • •

"You're a natural – a born natural!" said Robert Gladwin with wobbly-toned fatherly pride in his voice.

"Do you reckon?" asked Joe, his chest swelling with his achievement.

His eyes were fixed on the road and his hands were clutched slightly tighter on the wheel than they needed to be, but Joe had to admit he felt pretty comfortable with this driving business – far more than he thought he would.

"I've never known anyone get the hang of the clutch so quickly – it's always the sticking point for new drivers!"

Ahead of them was the hill that would take them to the top of the lane; and from there it was only a few minutes' drive home.

"I need to change down a gear for this hill, don't I?" Joe asked, his hearing already attuned to the noises and needs of the engine.

"Yes, well anticipated! Come down one gear now and be ready in case you feel like you need to slip down another as we come to the brow of the hill."

Joe's heart soared. He'd always got by at school all right, but it didn't come easy.

Being just about better than average doesn't really give you a buzz, he thought. *Not like drumming and not like this.*

"Good!" beamed his father as the car began its descent. "Now you need to – oh, look! It's Gillian and Kerry... Fancy showing them your driving skills and giving them a lift back home?"

"Sure!" said Joe, feeling around self-consciously for the indicator.

• • •

"Did you girls have a nice walk?"

"Oh, yes," Gillian replied to her partner's question from the back seat. "We had a lovely chat, didn't we, Kerry?"

Kerry nodded happily. A weight had been lifted from her shoulders: Gillian had put everything into perspective for her and as soon as she got back to town, she was going to phone Ollie and find out when she could see him to tell him what was going on.

Once that was done, it would be time to talk to her parents, which wouldn't be fun. But, as Gillian had said, saying nothing didn't make the problem go away.

Gazing out of the window, lost in her own thoughts for a second or two, Kerry was only dimly aware of Joe's dad merrily boasting about his son's driving skills.

How mean of me, she chastised herself instantly. *I haven't paid any attention to Joe...*

She turned to face forward and found her eyes drawn to the driver's mirror. Joe's soulful eyes were reflected there and, instead of looking ahead, they were – for that split second – staring straight back at her with an expression that gave Kerry a pang of *déjà vu*. And then it was gone. Joe's eyes followed the curve of the forest-enclosed road in front of him once again.

Kerry flipped her face around to the car window again and began twirling a curl around her finger as she racked her memory banks, trying hard to fix on what was familiar about that glance.

Her finger stopped, hair wound tight around it. She'd got it.

Ollie... she said to herself, memories of that amazing night at Matt's flooding back. That night last May when Ollie had joined her on the backdoor step, looked out across the star-lit garden with her, turned to her with *that look*, and then kissed her for the very first time...

But I must be wrong! Kerry felt her heart pitter-pattering. *It's not as if Joe's in love with me! Is it...?*

Gillian's scream might have shaken Kerry out of her muddled panic-stricken thoughts, but instead a sharp pain took her breath away and blackness overwhelmed her.

CHAPTER 20

• •

RALLYING ROUND

"Listen, I know I shouldn't be doing this, but I thought I'd better let you know that the others are on their way up here with a bit of surprise..."

"A surprise?" asked Kerry, wincing as she tried to make herself comfortable.

"In your condition, I don't think you need any more shocks or surprises," said Sonja, perched on the edge of the hospital bed. "But Ollie thinks it's a fantastic idea and it's supposed to cheer you up."

"Come on then – if you're going to spill the secret, then spill."

"Well, do you remember that today's Anna's birthday?"

Kerry's face went whiter than it already was – apart from the bruised purple swelling round her eye.

"Oh, no – I totally forgot! Poor Anna; I ruined her birthday..."

"Jeez, Kez! Of course you forgot – you were in a car crash yesterday!" Sonja teased her reassuringly. "Anyway, the surprise is that they're bringing her birthday party to your bedside!"

"I hope that really strict ward sister isn't on then – she shoos people away if there's any more than two visitors at a time. She did that last night when Mum and Dad were here with Ollie..."

"Don't worry – we'll have a two-by-two party if it comes to it!"

"But is everyone coming? I mean, what about the End?"

Sonja stared at her friend in amused disbelief. Kerry had a broken collarbone, two cracked ribs, a case of concussion and an eye that was going to come up as if she'd done five rounds with Prince Naseem.

And she's fretting about the work rota at the café? Sonja said to herself.

"Nick's got Irene and Dorothy in to help out so that Anna and Ollie could both come here this evening. Just relax! You have to be ready to act surprised in a minute..."

But Kerry still looked worried.

"Is Joe all right?"

"Yes, he's fine," nodded Sonja. "He's more or

less just bruised and achey. Same as his dad and Gillian."

From the frown on her forehead, Sonja could see that Kerry wasn't quite pacified.

"What happened to the deer?"

"Nothing – it just leapt away after it ran into the road."

"Honest?" said Kerry beseechingly.

"Honest. Why?"

"I thought Ollie was just trying to make me feel better when he told me Joe had swerved and missed it. I was scared it had been killed."

"Kez, the deer's off leaping around merrily in the woods somewhere, and Joe and his folks are fine. It's *you* that came off worst. You've got to concentrate on taking care of yourself!"

"But poor Joe – he must feel terrible..."

"Yeah, well, I don't think our Joey's that keen on jumping back behind the wheel too soon, that's for sure," shrugged Sonja. "But the accident shocked everyone, not just Joe."

"Did it?" asked Kerry, feeling a few tears prickling at her eyes.

"Course it did, you silly sausage!" said Sonja, moving up the bed and giving her friend a cuddle that made her wince again. "Ollie's been a wreck and me, well, it made me really think about things."

"Like?" asked Kerry with a little sniff.

"Like how it could have been a lot worse and that you've only got one life and you've got to make the most of it..."

"Sounds cheery," Kerry managed to laugh. "Ow!"

"No laughing! Think of those ribs!" Sonja chastised her, giggling herself. "But honestly, it has made me think. It's like, I've had this mad idea that I really want to go to uni near Owen, but I've been too shy to tell him – in case it sounds like I'm getting too serious. But I *am* going to tell him; I'm going to try and phone him later tonight."

Kerry's heart leapt at Sonja's words.

Why didn't she tell me before? And why didn't I think she'd understand what I've been going through?

"Son – it's funny you should say that 'cause I—"

"SURPRISE!!"

A bundle of faces and balloons appeared at the entrance to the little side ward and Kerry was quickly engulfed in arms and kisses.

"Happy Birthday, Anna – sorry you're having to celebrate it here!" Kerry apologised when she'd got her breath back.

"Hey, I'm not complaining!" smiled Anna.

"I've got friends, stupid balloons and even a cake..."

Cat pulled a cardboard cake box out of the carrier bag she was holding and flipped the lid up to show off the creamy flakes of chocolate decorating it as well as the nineteen candles stuck in.

"...but I do have one gripe with you."

Kerry looked perplexed. "What have I done, Anna?"

"Only ruined my New Year resolution. So much for a peaceful year – it's only the tenth of January and that resolution's blown already!"

"You can't just blame Kerry for that," laughed Ollie, perched at the head of the bed and holding his girlfriend's hand tightly. "Our Matt's been moping about being miserable all over the place, hasn't he? That's not very peaceful."

"Yeah, well, no more of that. Not after what's happened to you and Joe," said Matt, handing over a bunch of yellow roses to Kerry. "None of what went on with Gaby and me breaking up seems so bad after what you two have been through..."

"Joe?" said Kerry with a sudden urgency. The muddle of people and excitement around her were making her feel light-headed and, for a second, she couldn't make out his face.

"Kerry?"

She held out her hand to him and he shuffled forward shyly.

"I'm so sorry, Kerry. If I hadn't been driving..."

"Joe – it could have happened to anyone..." she protested.

"Yes and Jacques Villeneuve wouldn't have been able to do any better than *you* in those circumstances," Maya chipped in.

"Funny, though, isn't it?" Ollie grinned, trying to lighten the atmosphere. "There's your parents who don't want you riding on the back of my moped, Kez, and the time you up and get hurt, you're in the back of a nice, respectable hatchback!"

"Um, Ollie, I don't think that remark's exactly going to make your mate here feel any better!" scolded Maya, wrapping an arm around Joe.

Joe shrugged, knowing that Ollie didn't mean anything. Even if he had, Joe was too lost in his own guilt to have noticed.

I could have killed her, he repeated to himself as he had done ever since he'd stumbled from his dad's car the previous afternoon. *How could I have looked Ollie in the eye ever again after that!*

He gazed at the way Ollie was entwined protectively around Kerry, how he kissed her fingers and gently stroked her hair away from her face.

I don't have to give up loving Kerry, Joe realised all of a sudden. *I just have to love her in a different way from Ollie. I have to love her as a friend...*

Cat, mistaking Joe's silence for pain at Ollie's dig, tried to change the subject with a little light gossip.

"Hey, Kez, did you know that Maya's a total heartbreaker now? She's just driving men off – including mine, I have to say."

"Cat! That's not quite true!" Maya protested, aware that she was being teased.

"Yes it is! I got a visit from Marc yesterday – seems Rudi's so gutted at being turned down by Ms Fussypants here..."

"Oh!" tsked Maya.

"...that he's decided to cut short his stay in Britain and head back home to Holland. And Marc's going too!"

Kerry put her hand protectively on her sides and tried not to laugh. But at the same time, she again felt that strange tug of *déjà vu*.

What has that story reminded me of? she wondered. *Rudi falling for Maya... is it that?*

Suddenly, the vision of Joe's eyes flashed through her mind – framed in the driver's mirror of his dad's car. Beseeching eyes that seemed desperate to tell her something.

How crazy am I? she thought, wriggling with embarrassment and feeling her ribs protest. *How bigheaded am I to think Joe fancies me?*

She turned her head and looked into Ollie's eyes. He was the only boy who fancied her and she was more than happy – completely ecstatic – with that.

"All right, Kerry?" he whispered, giving her hand a squeeze.

"Oh, yes," she smiled at him.

It's true what Sonja was saying about this whole accident sorting things out in your mind, she thought, squeezing his hand right back. *And now I know I've done the right thing...*

Her mind drifted to the pile of unsent university applications stashed in the bottom of her wardrobe in the chewed plastic bag.

Now all I've got to do is keep my fingers crossed that the college in the city accepts me. If I get that and I've got Ollie, then I really will be happy, just like I wished for at New Year...

Sugar
SECRETS...

...& Scandal

SNEAK PREVIEW!

"Hey, Billy boy – what do you reckon to this?"

Nick slapped a pink piece of paper on the Formica table top, flopped down on to the seat opposite and waited for a response.

Billy looked at the A5 sheet and didn't know what to say. There was an old-fashioned drawing on it, of what Billy guessed was supposed to be a Bunny Girl, beside black printed words which read: 'Pretty Ladies – the Escort Agency for the discerning gentleman. Discretion guaranteed. Phone today on...'

Billy was stumped. Maybe Nick – with his ponytail 'n' bald spot combo, and penchant for old rock T-shirts – wasn't *every* girl's idea of a dream date, but he never seemed to have any difficulty turning on the charm and chatting up women in the Railway Tavern, when he wasn't busy watching his protégés play. So why did he need to get involved in something as seedy as an escort agency?

"Nick – call for you!" Anna shouted across the café, holding the receiver of the wall phone up in the air.

"'Scuse," said Nick, grabbing up the pink slip of paper and striding off.

Billy sank into the seat with relief. He'd broken out into a sweat wondering what to say that wasn't along the lines of, "What are you – a dirty old man?"

But he wasn't out of trouble yet; Nick could finish his call and be back over just as quickly, and there was still no sign of Ollie. Billy wished like crazy that he hadn't decided to take a detour to come and meet Ollie after he'd finished his shift. He should have just made his way straight to The Swan, as he did every Tuesday evening, ready for the band rehearsal in the back room of Ollie's folks' pub.

He tried to catch Anna's eye – to ask her if Ollie was nearly through in the kitchen – when he was saved by the arrival of Kerry and Sonja.

"What are you doing here? Isn't it your practice night tonight?" asked Sonja, slipping in beside him and pinching a crisp from his open packet.

"Yeah, it is," nodded Billy, offering the packet to Kerry. "I'm just waiting for Ollie. I thought I'd come by for him since I was visiting a mate round the corner."

Billy wondered if he should tell the girls about what Nick had shown him, but he decided to save it for Ollie. Nick was his uncle, after all.

"Here's Ollie now," Kerry found herself smiling as she watched him bound through from the doorway that led to the kitchen. It was always the same when she caught sight of her boyfriend, no matter how long they'd been going out. That strange sense of shyness and bliss all rolled into one tingly, happy feeling that bubbled up inside her.

"Hey, gorgeous," said Ollie, before burrowing his face into the dark reddish curls that hid Kerry's neck, half kissing, half tickling her.

"Get off!" she giggled, pushing him gently away.

"Come on, Sonja – your turn!" he joked, leaning over as if he was about to give her the same treatment.

"Don't you dare!" yelped Sonja, holding her friend at arm's length.

As he laughingly watched the two of them tussling, Billy's eyes were suddenly drawn beyond them, to the dark-haired girl with the pierced nose who was sitting by the jukebox with her mate. And just like Sunday – as Joe had pointed out – her eyes seemed glued to Ollie.

Weird, thought Billy, though he was still more agitated by Nick's sudden interest in the escort agency.

"Have the girls told you about their amazing psychic readings on Sunday?" Ollie distracted him by asking, now that the play fight was over.

"No," Billy shook his head.

"Don't worry – you haven't missed out on much," grinned Sonja. "The only amazing thing about them was how *bad* they all were."

"Yeah?" said Billy, without much surprise. He didn't believe in all that spiritual stuff anyway. He liked things straightforward, simple and up front.

"Well, they weren't *all* bad," Kerry reminded her best friend. "Maya's was pretty amazing!"

"How come?" Billy quizzed her, now intrigued.

Billy had a soft spot for Maya; had even asked her out on a date when he'd first known her, but it hadn't worked out. Maya didn't seem to see him as anything more than friend material. But while he wasn't holding his breath or losing sleep over it, Billy – a born optimist – often wondered if she'd change her mind at any point in the future. He certainly wouldn't complain if she did.

"It was really accurate about her family and her personality and everything..."

"Yeah, but skip to the interesting part, Kez!" urged Sonja.

"Well," said Kerry, her hazel eyes widening behind her wire-rimmed specs. "She was told that there's going to be a new chapter in her life – a big change – and it's all to do with love..."

"Really?" said Billy, raising his eyebrows.

Maybe, he thought to himself, *just maybe I shouldn't be so cynical about all this psychic stuff after all...*

CAN YOU HANDLE SCANDAL?

• •

When scandal threatens Maya and Ollie, they handle it in very different ways. Maya's about to fall slap bang in love with someone she probably shouldn't. Ollie, meanwhile, has the opposite problem – but it's just as much of a dilemma. And what dodginess is Nick up to now?

How would you face up to the worst kind of gossip? Take our test and see how you'd score...

(1) You hear that someone you only vaguely know has been in trouble with the police. How does it make you feel?

a) Curious, but guilty for listening to gossip. You'd like to hear their side of the story.

b) Only mildly interested – with you, gossip about people you don't have any connection with just goes in one ear and out the other.

c) Tantalised – you want to hear more, so you can get the story straight when you pass it on!

(2) You hear a rumour about one of your friends. The rumour says that they've been making crank calls to one of the teachers. How does that make you feel?

a) Concerned for them, but you plan to lend your support; to back them up if the story's not true, and give them help and advice if it is.

b) Concerned, but embarrassed. You wish you could find out it's not true and that everything would go back to the way it was.

c) Concerned for them, but excited too. After all, there's nothing like a bit of gossip to brighten up the day!

(3) Uh-oh – you hear that people are saying you've been snogging your best friend's boyfriend! It's absolutely not true. How does that make you feel?

a) Horrified – but you're made of tough stuff; you'll deal with it.

b) Mortified – all you can think about is that you wish it would go away.

c) Shocked – but chuffed to be the centre of attention.

(4) Your friend's diary is lying open and you see your own name written there. Would you read on?

a) No way. You wouldn't want anyone to look in your diary, so you wouldn't do it to anyone else.

b) Maybe, even though you knew you'd feel terrible about it.

c) Absolutely. After all, who could resist finding out her innermost secrets, especially when they're about you!

(5) Someone sidles up to you and asks if the rumour about why your mate keeps taking time off to go to the doctor is true. It is, and you know all the gory details. Of course, you don't tell...

a) ...because it's no one else's business.

b) ...but you feel uncomfortable knowing stuff you can't talk about.

c) ...but it makes you feel kind of smug knowing that you're in on the secret and they're not.

6) In class, someone passes you a note with an eye-boggling story about what one of your friends got up to at a party at the weekend. It sounds totally made up. You:

a) Read it, shove it in your pocket, and vow to stick it in a bin at the soonest opportunity.

b) Try not to look at it, and pass the horrible note on to the next person as quick as you can. You don't want anything to do with it.

c) Giggle at what it says, and pass it on.

7) Strolling along the road one day, you suddenly spot your mate gazing slushy-eyed at a boy she's never had anything to do with before. You think:

a) There could be a simple explanation. Maybe she's looking for a bit of dust in his contact lens.

b) You'd better get out of there fast, in case you see something you shouldn't.

c) You've rumbled a full-scale secret romance!

8) Your best friend tells you a super-sensitive secret. There's no way...

a) ...you'd breath a word of it to anyone else. However uncomfortable, it's for your ears only, unless she tells you different.

b) ...you'd tell anyone. But you feel practically crippled with the burden of this secret.

c) ...you could keep something *that* gossip-worthy to yourself. You've got to spill!

(9) Oops – you've been snogging someone you shouldn't and you think someone's spotted you. It's the sort of thing that would whiz round your school like wildfire if the story got out. What do you do?

a) Start working out what to say and do if the rumours start flying. Having a good answer will spoil the gossips' fun.

b) Pretend nothing's happened – and pray that you don't have to end up locking yourself in your room for a year till the rumours die down.

c) Let people gossip if they want to – you don't care!

(10) Someone you're not remotely interested in fancies you, and they're making a right fool of themselves. Everyone's talking about it. What do you do?

a) Try to put a stop to it by talking to the person and telling them it's not on, or get a trustworthy friend to do it for you.

b) Ignore the person at all costs and hope they'll get bored and give up.

c) Nothing – after all, it does your reputation no harm to seem so popular!

NOW CHECK OUT HOW YOU SCORED...

SO, HOW DO YOU HANDLE SCANDAL?

● ●

Mostly a

You're sensitive and ultra-smart, and whether scandal is aimed at you or others, you know just how to handle it: with dollops of sense and tact. Not that you seek out scandal in any way; like Maya, you much prefer things to be straightforward and simple. But when trouble comes a-creeping you know the honourable thing to do.

Mostly b

When trouble's brewin', you make like a bird. An ostrich to be exact, sticking your head in the sand. You hate when things get all nasty and problematic, and like Ollie, your immediate reaction is to smile sweetly, ignore it, and hope the whole thing goes away. Least said, soonest mended sometimes works – but don't count your chickens!

Mostly c

Hmm – you're not the sensitive 'n' smart type like Maya, but you're not the shy-away type like Ollie either. You are – we have to say it – a total tact-free zone; someone who gets a kick from scandal, whether it relates to other people or to you – even when it's only in your own mind! Better beware – you react just like Cat!

Sugar
SECRETS...
...& Revenge

LOVE!
Cat's in love with the oh-so-gorgeous
Matt and don't her friends know it.

HUMILIATION!
Then he's caught snogging Someone
Else at Ollie's party.

REVENGE!
Watch out Matt – Cat's claws are out...

Meet the whole crowd in the first ever
episode of Sugar Secrets.

*Some secrets are just too good to
keep to yourself!*

Collins
An Imprint of HarperCollins*Publishers*
www.fireandwater.com

Sugar
SECRETS...
...& Rivals

FRIENDS!
Kerry can count on Sonja – they've been best friends forever.

BETRAYAL!
Then Ollie's sister turns up and things just aren't the same.

RIVALS!
How can Kerry possibly hope to compete with the glamorous Natasha?

Some secrets are just too good to keep to yourself!

Collins
An Imprint of HarperCollinsPublishers
www.fireandwater.com

Sugar
SECRETS...
...& Lies

CONFESSIONS!
Is Ollie in love? Yes? No? Definitely maybe!

THE TRUTH!
Sonja is determined to find out who the lucky girl can be.

LIES!
But someone's not being honest, which might just break Kerry's heart...

Some secrets are just too good to keep to yourself!

Collins
An Imprint of HarperCollinsPublishers
www.fireandwater.com

Sugar
SECRETS...
...& Freedom

FAMILIES!
They can drive you insane, and Maya's
at breaking point with hers.

GUILT!
There's tragedy in store – but is Joe
partly to blame?

FREEDOM!
The price is high, so who's going
to pay...?

Some secrets are just too good to
keep to yourself!

Collins
An Imprint of HarperCollinsPublishers
www.fireandwater.com

Sugar
SECRETS...
...& Mistakes

MATES!
Should they become dates? That's the
question on everyone's lips.

CRASH!
Matt surprises everyone by falling slap-
bang, flat-on-his-face in love.

MISTAKES!
But things are not quite as they seem.
Has he landed himself in trouble?

*Some secrets are just too good to
keep to yourself!*

Collins
An Imprint of HarperCollinsPublishers
www.fireandwater.com

Sugar
SECRETS...
...& Choices

CRISIS!
Kerry and Ollie are a couple behaving
strangely – and Joe is taking notes...

SEX!
It's definitely in the air, and it seems to
be affecting everybody!

CHOICES!
Is it the end of everything or the start of
something new? One thing's for sure –
it's decision time!

*Some secrets are just too good to
keep to yourself!*

Collins
An Imprint of HarperCollinsPublishers
www.fireandwater.com

Sugar
SECRETS...
...& Ambition

GIRLS!
Matt's surrounded by them – but why
are they making him so nervous?

TENSION!
An unexpected party guest stirs up old
resentments and sets Sonja thinking
about her future.

AMBITION!
Sonja's aiming for The Top, but will she
have any friends left when she gets there?

*Some secrets are just too good to
keep to yourself!*

Collins
An Imprint of HarperCollinsPublishers
www.fireandwater.com

Sugar
SECRETS...
...& Dramas

PARTY PARTY!
Seems like everyone's having fun.
Everyone except Anna, that is...

SCHEMES!
Matt and the others are making plans –
but will their dreams come true?

DRAMAS!
Cat's really acting up again – and this
time she's having a ball!

*Some secrets are just too good to
keep to yourself!*

Collins
An Imprint of HarperCollinsPublishers
www.fireandwater.com

Order Form

To order direct from the publishers, just make a list of the titles you want and fill in the form below:

Name ....

Address ....

....

....

Send to: Dept 6, HarperCollins Publishers Ltd, Westerhill Road, Bishopbriggs, Glasgow G64 2QT.

Please enclose a cheque or postal order to the value of the cover price, plus:

UK & BFPO: Add £1.00 for the first book, and 25p per copy for each additional book ordered.

Overseas and Eire: Add £2.95 service charge. Books will be sent by surface mail but quotes for airmail despatch will be given on request.

A 24-hour telephone ordering service is available to Visa and Access card holders: 0141- 772 2281

Collins
An *Imprint of* HarperCollins*Publishers*